RED RED ROSE

"What the hell do you think you're doing?" a deep voice demanded, only inches from her ear.

She wanted to respond, to say something witty and clever—something to distract him from her real purpose. Her throat felt as if it were closing, her mouth full of cotton. She looked toward the voice. His face was in the shadows, as was hers. Probably a beat cop pulling this assignment as some sort of punishment. Just a guard. Obviously, not one of the inner circle—not familiar with the faces of the men and women in the detective division or their outside experts. Sure, why not go for it? She croaked out the first thing that popped into her mind. "Let go of my arm. Who are you to question me? I'm here on official business, and unless you wish to be cited for obstruction, I suggest you go back to your post." There—it was out. Now, to see if it worked.

"Mind if I take a look at your badge?"

"Mind if I see yours?"

She could imagine him smiling at her in the darkness, knowing she was bluffing. He flashed something in front of her that looked official. She gave it a cursory glance without bothering to read, rapidly planning her next move.

"Now, it's your turn."

"I don't carry a badge," she replied, using her most intimidating tone. "I am a criminal profiler on special assignment. Now, if you don't mind—it's late, and I have a lot of work to do."

"Sorry to have bothered you, Ms. I don't believe I caught your name."

"Quite all right. You were just doing your job. And as we're not likely to cross paths again, I find the exchange of our names to be pointless. Don't you?" Tucking the note under her arm, she walked away, hoping the stranger would follow her example. When she had gone far enough to feel safe, she risked a look back. He was gone. Relief washed over her with the suddenness of a spring shower. Moving as quickly as possible without attracting attention, she returned the note to the Chief's car and headed for the Ghia. Never had the little car looked so good.

She turned the key and found the road without benefit of her lights, thankful an unexpected pothole had not swallowed her up. About a hundred feet from where she had parked, she risked illumination. Yes. She had done it. Excitement coursed through her like a good wine. She had penetrated a crime scene, conducted an investigation under the noses of the veteran detectives, and no one was the wiser. What could be better than this? She pulled off the main road absorbed in her thoughts, unaware of the narrowed pair of eyes patiently watching her exit.

Red Red Rose

Other novels by C. Rowe–Myers

Black Ice/Shadowed Road

Through the Shadows (a Black Ice novel)

Red Red Rose

An Augustus Mallory Mystery

C. Rowe–Myers

iUniverse, Inc.
New York Lincoln Shanghai

Red Red Rose

An Augustus Mallory Mystery

All Rights Reserved © 2003 by C. Rowe–Myers

No part of this book may be reproduced or transmitted in any form or by any means, graphic, electronic, or mechanical, including photocopying, recording, taping, or by any information storage retrieval system, without the written permission of the publisher.

iUniverse, Inc.

For information address:
iUniverse, Inc.
2021 Pine Lake Road, Suite 100
Lincoln, NE 68512
www.iuniverse.com

ISBN: 0-595-30266-1

Printed in the United States of America

This novel is dedicated to my wonderful family—who supported me while I pounded this novel out under a deadline. Also—a big *thanks* to Sally, whose watchful eye studied every line and every dot. And—a big *thanks* to Lyn, whose beautiful art graces the cover of this book.

RED RED ROSE

Roses are red;
Violets are blue.
When death is final
I think of you.

CHAPTER 1

▼

She watched the rose petals fall one by one into the ruby river of blood, floating like little red boats seeking safety—harbor—absolution. She winced for the dying girl lying unconscious on the grass—broken. Recoiled at the horror, the waste—the butchery. Rivulets of scarlet marring pale skin, designing a map to nowhere—directions to death—to God.

She looked at the man. He was God—a god—the god—her god—scattering petals over her body like a shroud. A tiny moan escaped from her lips and fled. More roses, more petals, last breath—scene from a late-night B movie, fading into the credits. Poor roses, poor girl, poor her.

Chief Detective Augustus Mallory woke up to the sound of squirrels chattering across the yard—warning the visiting cat of their anger and ferocity. Turning over, he covered his head with a pillow. Damn nuisances. His one day to sleep late. The move to East Texas had been exhausting and the precinct transfer—tedious. How much paperwork did the government need to relocate a man? A great deal—if the forms he had filled out last week were any indication.

"Shoo. Shoo. No, cat. Go home. Git," Maria shouted, before lapsing into a tirade of unintelligible Spanish. Maria Consuello, Mallory's long-time housekeeper, had squirrel feeders set up all around the yard and didn't tolerate any animals that threatened her adopted pets.

Mallory tossed the covers to the side of the bed. Might as well get up. Maria's coffee would be worth the effort—its rich flavor the one thing he could count on in life. He was in the middle of his second cup when the phone rang, putting an end to any thoughts of living the weekend away from the station.

2   Red Red Rose

"Mallory here."

"Sorry to call you on a Saturday, Detective, but something's come up. Something you're going to want to see for yourself, given your interest in the Gerald case."

"Another body?"

"Yes. Same MO as before."

He shook his head, dragging his hand across the back of his neck. "I was afraid of this. Was there a note?"

"In the right pant pocket."

"Don't move anything. I'm on my way." Mallory wrote down the address and downed his last swallow of coffee. He was leaving the kitchen just as Maria was coming in.

"Dratted cats. We need a fence. A six foot fence would protect my squirrels."

"Fences won't keep cats out of the yard."

Maria looked up in surprise. "Then, we'll get an electric fence. That will."

"Probably hurt more squirrels than cats, Maria. The cats will just climb the trees over the fence and drop down into the yard. Besides, we need the cats. Been thinking about getting a couple as pets."

"No. No cats. Why would you want cats?"

"To keep the snakes away."

Maria stopped and turned. "Snakes? Are there many snakes in East Texas?"

Mallory pressed his advantage. "Hundreds. A few cats might be a good idea." He left the kitchen before Maria could continue the conversation, heading straight for his study. He would have enjoyed baiting her further, but what awaited him in his desk drawer was far more serious than a few poisonous snakes. Opening the bottom drawer he withdrew a file entitled *Rose* and sat down.

The color photograph lying on top was graphic—gruesome—a salute to the concept of bizarre. Yet, somehow it was also compelling—a work of dark art. He lifted the eight by ten glossy out of the file to take a closer look. The clues were in the details, giving him a subtle glimpse into the mind of the murderer. The use of red rose petals, coupled with the notes was the most significant aspect of the case, but the care with which the murderer displayed the victim was also revealing. Tandy Gerald was the first, but he knew she wouldn't be the last. The writing assured him of that. The killer was on a mission—a crusade—and murder was only one step in the process—not the end goal.

He stared at the photographs of the crime scene. The body was nude but not bare. From the neck down to the legs, the victim was covered in red petals from hybrid tea roses. The stems of the flowers had been braided into a crown of thorns and placed on the girl's head. Beneath the makeshift wreath, her hair had been styled, and fresh makeup had been applied to her face. According to the coroner she had been knocked unconscious before any of this took place—before she was cut with a small knife. Intricate designs revolving around the letter "A" had been carved into her skin like red tattoos. Death had occurred several hours later from loss of blood. She had not been sexually assaulted and her clothes were folded neatly beside her. Inside the neat pile of garments was where they found the note. He pulled the writing from the folder.

My love is like a red, red…
Up from the grave she arose.
Strains from a moldy-smelling hymn book
Haunt my life and color my dreams
Resurrecting ghosts—her ghost—my red rose.

Petals floating on the breeze
Falling, falling, falling
Spilling my red rose
Seeping her into the soil
Nourishing the earth
Leaving me deserted—
A desert of thorns and rusting leaves.

I bleed.
You bleed.
We all bleed.
Ring around the rosy.
I, too, will feed the earth she loved.
Drip blood upon the rose.

*   *   *   *

Pagan ground her cigarette out in the ashtray, expelling the last puff of smoke from her lungs. Damn cancer sticks. Why couldn't she just give them up? Adult thumb sucking—that's what her shrink had called it. She called it survival. God, just thinking about giving them up made her want another one. She uncrossed her long, slender legs and stood up. At five foot eleven, she had to duck under the hanging plant to walk down the steps of the travel trailer she called home. Her uncle called it her turtle shell—at least, that was one of the things he called it—one of his nicer names for her little nest.

Hell's bells—why shouldn't she carry her home on her back? Better than being tied to a house. She re-tied her halter-top and twisted her long, brown hair into a knot on top of her head. Would this heat never let up? Texas in July was setting new records in humidity. Wet heat. Free sauna for everyone. God only knew what August would be like. Sliding into the seat of her neon yellow Karmann Ghia, she headed toward the one-horse town of Nelsonville to feed her second serious addiction—Diet Coke. No, third. Coffee definitely came in second, but she had that back at the house.

She was sitting at the only four-way stop—applying her lipstick—when she realized it was her turn to go. Unfortunately, the man sitting beside her had the same thought and hit the gas. The collision was inevitable, but not serious—more embarrassing than damaging, with the major injury to the bumpers rather than the bodies of the cars. After the first stun of impact, she felt anger overcoming her sense of relief. Her exit from the car was enthusiastic—goaded by feelings of righteous indignation.

"Excuse me," she said, approaching the man in the new Lexus. "I believe I clearly had the right-of-way. Just because you happen to own an expensive car, you think you own the road as well. Your license and proof of insurance, please," she finished, holding out her hand.

The man opened his door, forcing her back to avoid another impact with his vehicle. She took an additional step backwards as he unfolded his 6'4" frame to tower above her.

"I take it you're not hurt," he opened, ignoring her earlier remarks. "Your lipstick looks to be on straight—that is what you seemed to be concerned with at the time. I'm new to the state and didn't realize stop signs were appropriate places to apply face paint. Do you people take the opportunity to bathe at them as well?"

Her eyes narrowed, then widened as she broke into a broad grin. "I could have you lynched for a remark like that, you know. And for your information, my right to put on makeup anywhere I deem appropriate is my privilege as a woman not as a Texan." She walked to the front of the car. "We don't seem to have sustained any significant damage, and I need a drink." Ignoring him, she climbed back into her car and started the engine.

"Don't I get a say in this?"

"As it was my turn, you broke the law, not me. I am the injured party, so I get to say if we carry this further or not. I say not. Goodbye."

"Let me buy you a drink."

"No, thanks," she said, leaving him in a cloud of dust.

The drive into the country was pleasant, the charm of the scenic roadway giving no hint of the horror waiting beyond its paved outlines. Mallory was loath to trade the vibrant array of life around him for the picture of death awaiting him at the end of the road—no matter how artfully displayed. A circle of flashing parked patrol cars signaled the area of the crime scene. As soon as he stopped the car, an officer approached and led him to the body.

The dead woman was laid out like royalty. Her long, blonde hair fanned out around her face—magazine cover posed. The entire scene was marginally surreal—a children's book of fairy tales baptized with the blood of a Poe protagonist. The rose petals, however, were the real anomaly. The beauty of the picture made the murder seem even more tragic—less comprehensible.

"Detective Mallory." Mallory looked up at the man coming toward him.

"Chief Redford."

"When did the call come in?"

"About an hour ago."

"Who found her?"

"James Tucker, a worker on the ranch. He was repairing a section of fence when the red color caught his attention. He thought a cow had been slaughtered."

Mallory looked at the small pile of clothes beside the body. "And the note?"

Redford handed him a piece of paper protected by an evidence bag. The words were clearly written.

"Come into my garden," said the serpent to the lass.
"I'll pick for you a scented rose;
You'll sit upon my lap.
We'll make love on a petalled bed
A crown of thorns you'll wear
And I will crush the sweet perfume
Into your yellow hair.

You'll sing a song of sorrow
I'll anoint you with my love.
Even God will cry real tears
As he watches from above.
And as the light fades from your eyes—
Your warm skin growing cold
I'll worship you, my lovely girl—
Become my red, red rose."

*   *   *   *

"Interesting."

"Is that your literary review, Mallory?"

Mallory looked up. "The feel of this poem is different from the first one. In fact, everything about the two poems is different."

"Are you thinking that we're dealing with a copycat?"

"How could we be? The fact there was a poem at the first murder scene was never released. It wasn't, was it?"

"No."

"Then unless it was one of us…" He let his voice drift off. "I believe the killer is the same, but that the differences are significant. We can either figure out the riddles or wait for number three."

"You think there will be a number three?"

Mallory nodded. "I think there will be a number twenty if we don't stop him."

Redford looked surprised. "You're serious. You think we have a bona fide serial killer on our hands, don't you? Wow. Who'da thought? This could be big—real big. There's liable to be national coverage on a story like this. Sure, why not? I should prepare a formal statement."

Mallory watched Redford's eyes light up and swell like a patron in a flea market with dreams of finding hidden treasure. Interviews, talk shows, tea with the governor—his ambition knew no bounds. If the Chief had his way, the entire scene would be a media circus before nightfall. So much for solving the case.

Mallory shrugged. "Of course, all publicity isn't good, is it?"

"What do you mean?"

"Well, if the police work is sloppy or the crime scene polluted, the reporters will tear us apart. They will say we botched the case. We might even be held in some way responsible for any subsequent killings."

"Damn. I hadn't thought of that. What do you think we should do?"

"Our job—quietly and efficiently—with as little outside contact as possible. The fewer people who know the specific details of the crime at this stage, the better."

"So, we still don't mention the notes?"

"Absolutely not."

"And the roses?"

"We will try to keep all details of the crime from the media for as long as possible."

"That won't be easy. Too many people involved."

"Well, do the best you can. If you'll excuse me now, I'd like to take some notes at the scene."

"Of course."

Mallory returned to the body for another look. As in the first case, meticulous care had been taken in the display of the victim. Careful not to touch the hair, Mallory squatted down beside the head to take a closer look at the woman's face. Her fair skin had been covered in makeup and a light powdered substance that seemed to shimmer in the light. Although not sure about the foundation makeup, he was sure the shimmer stuff had been applied by the killer. Sure, because minute bits of it had fallen on the petals near her face.

The eyes were open—staring. Deep blue eye shadow, topped by a hint of bronze, covered the lids. The entire eye had been outlined with a thick, black line, mimicking an Egyptian hieroglyph. The strokes were much too heavy for the woman's delicate blonde coloring. Not something she would have chosen for herself. At least, that was his impression. The eyelashes were thick and long. Too thick—too long. He touched the end of one with the tip of his pen. Ah ha. They were fake—glued on to the edge of the lid to appear real. Wonder how much time that took?

Blush had been applied to the cheeks, and the lips were outlined and painted in a brighter hue. The careful coloring gave the impression of life to the dead woman, keeping her alive for the artist. The artist? Is that what this man was? So, how did he preserve his art? Not enough time to paint the model on canvas. So, the killer must keep his art alive through photography. Which would mean he must develop his own prints—not an usual hobby or an inexpensive one.

Mallory picked up one of the petals from beside the body. Why roses? Their beauty? Their fragrance? No. Mallory had the feeling it was something else—that the flowers had some special significance for the killer? But what? When he knew that, he would probably know the identity of the killer.

CHAPTER 2

▼

Pagan Mallory pulled into the parking lot of the convenience store, throwing open the car door before the last notes had died on the radio. The narrowed looks she got from the people at the gas pumps told her they would prefer hearing something other than the rhythmic chant of Slim Shady assaulting the quiet Texas morning. Oh well. She tossed them a fleeting glimpse of her most charming smile before striding defiantly into the busy store, unaware of the many admiring looks cast in her direction.

Labeled "skinny" most of her early life and "bean pole" in her later years, she was not really conscious of how striking she appeared to the general populace. Oh, she knew she was attractive—pretty even, with her curtain of butt length brown hair swaying behind her back, but she would never have considered herself to be a beauty. She set the Diet Coke on the counter. Wasn't counting calories—just liked the taste.

"That be all for ya?"

"Yeah, I'm trying to quit."

The cryptic remark earned her a blank stare. "Huh, I didn't even know Diet Coke was bad for ya. My sister drinks them all the time."

She picked up her change before the subject digressed to an even lower level and headed for the door. Outside, the sun was blindingly bright, causing her to scramble madly inside her bag for her sunglasses. Strong arms reached out to steady her before she plowed headlong into a red high-lift pickup blocking her path.

"Whoa, there."

10   Red Red Rose

"Oh, I'm sorry." She had to shade her eyes to look up into the stranger's face. "Didn't see you for the bright sun." She squinted, trying to see under the ten-gallon hat. Not that she was overly curious. Like a lot of Texas women, she had learned to avoid cowboys at an early age. Most of them were hard to rope, hard to hold, and definitely not in touch with their feminine sides. She preferred her men with more of a preppie look.

"Yeah, it sure is that. Blind ya if ya don't watch out. Some people avoid that by putting on their sunglasses before they leave the building. You might try it."

She lifted her eyebrows in surprise, trying even harder to peer under the hat. The words delivered in that deadpan Texas drawl were definitely not what she had expected to hear. "Yeah, I'll try that next time. Thanks for the advice."

"Anytime," he said, sidestepping her to the door.

Pagan slipped behind the wheel of the car she usually referred to simply as Ghia, taking a big swig of her low calorie drink. The squat little automobile appeared even smaller beside the oversized truck. If the lifters had been any higher, she could have driven under the truck instead of around it. Throwing the car into gear, she backed out, and darted onto the highway. She was two miles down the road before she remembered the man in the Lexus. Now, there was a man she needed to get to know—not a man in a cowboy hat.

By the time she reached her uncle's house, she was ready for a nap. Not that it was a long trip, twenty miles at the outside. It was the heat. Texas heat was made for sleeping. She planned to take a long dip in the pool, drink some of Maria's cold ice tea, and then stretch out for a snooze. By then, her uncle should be home from work.

Mallory walked into his private office and shut the door. He needed some time to be alone—to think—to let the facts run around in his head until they fell into a coherent order. He looked at the most recent glossies of the murdered girl. They didn't—couldn't do justice to the horrific scene he had just witnessed. Reaching into the file folder, he removed the pictures of the first scene, lining them up side by side. As alike as they appeared to be, there were differences—subtle differences. These peculiarities were what he found to be of interest. He got out his notes.

He was about to begin a list when a knock at the door interrupted him. "Come in."

"Mallory, I hate to disturb you, but there is someone I'd like you to meet."

Always the gentleman, Detective Mallory laid down his pen and stood—out of respect to the ladies. Gail Whiting, one of the few female detectives on staff, brought forward another female—decidedly not on staff. Why was he so sure? It was the look of her. A woman not used to taking orders—not used to being supervised—not used to being in the company of rowdy men.

"Mallory, this is Theodora Van Zandt, our consulting criminal psychologist. She will be assisting us in the investigation. Theo, this is Chief Detective Augustus Mallory. He is in charge of the case."

Theo offered her hand, and Mallory took it in a firm clasp. "Nice to meet you, Ms. Van Zandt."

"Please, Chief Detective, call me Theo."

He smiled. "All right, Theo. Most people call me Mallory."

She smiled in return. "Does anyone call you Mal?"

His smile faltered a little. "I had a friend who used to."

"Sorry, didn't mean to pry."

"That's okay. We've lost touch, that's all. Won't you have a seat?"

As she sat down, Whiting excused herself from the room.

"Quite an interesting case."

"You've read the reports, then?"

"Yes, I read about the latest murder just a few minutes ago. Of course, everything's not in yet."

"No, but enough to determine that these are unusual cases. Did you visit either crime scene?"

"Unfortunately, no. I didn't have the opportunity. I became officially involved in the case about ten minutes ago. Did you?"

"Yes, both of them."

"Hm...." She reached over to pick up the photographs from the desk.

Mallory gave her a closer look. Fortyish, smartly dressed in a beige suit, hair secured in a demure twist, neat, attractive—just what he would have expected her to look like. He wondered what she wore when she wasn't at work. She laid the photos back down.

"So, what did you see that the photos didn't show? Your main impressions?"

Mallory glanced at the still shots and thought back to the scenes. "Murder is a dirty, ugly business. Art is supposed to be beautiful, uplifting—exalting. In the murderer's mind, they are one and the same. To me, that is what makes this case so disturbing. The killer sees the horror of death as a part of his creativity—his expression of beauty."

"The scene was beautiful?"

"If you could ignore the fact the centerpiece was a corpse. Yes, the site was aesthetically pleasing. Attention given to every detail."

12   Red Red Rose

She pointed to the photos. "The girls appear to be wearing makeup? Was it pre or post-mortem?"

"Postmortem."

"Interesting."

Mallory opened the folder. "Have you read his poetry?"

Theo smiled. "Yes, I have. Interesting. Not particularly literary but revealing, nevertheless. A writer as well as an artist. I have to wonder if he is published—teaching, maybe. Did this single act fulfill his vision or is he selecting his next victim even as we speak?"

Mallory was wondering the same thing.

By the time Mallory arrived home that evening, the sun was still sitting gloriously above the horizon. Maria met him at the door full of smiles. He glanced covertly at his watch. No, he wasn't early. In fact, he was well past the time that would have normally earned him the sharp side of her tongue. He looked around for some clue as to the cause of her good mood. Nothing. But he didn't have long to guess because Maria was bursting to tell him.

"Pagan's here," she said, pleased as a cat eating a canary.

Ah, that explained it. His niece was one of Maria's favorite people. Sometimes, he thought the only reason Maria had agreed to follow him to East Texas was to be near Pagan. If Pagan had been here for any length of time Maria probably had the entire kitchen filled with baked goods. Not that the girl ever ate them. Steak was more her style. Hearty appetite for one so thin—like having a teenage boy around the house instead of a twenty-five year old woman.

"Let me guess. She's in the pool."

Maria fairly beamed. "Been here all afternoon. Said she might stay a few days."

"What about her job? She didn't quit, did she?"

"She said she's using her sick leave."

Mallory shook his head. "They don't give sick leave to temps, Maria. Sounds like she's playing hooky."

"Now, don't you go fussin' at her. We're just glad she's here. I'm sure she has a perfectly good reason for not being at work."

"That's the problem, Maria. I'm sure she has, too."

Maria led the way to the pool, intent on protecting her young charge from any verbal chastisement from her uncle. She needn't have worried. Although he had tried on more than one occasion, Mallory was no more capable of staying mad at Pagan than he had been at her father, his brother, when they were growing up.

"Uncle Mal. I'm so glad you're home. Give me a minute to get changed, and then there is something very important I have to talk to you about. Okay? Be right out."

He watched her disappear into the changing room. Last time she had wanted to talk to him, it had cost him five thousand dollars and a year's supply of magazine subscriptions. That was when she had wanted to open the magazine/purse shop. *Mags and Bags*—she had called it. That had lasted about eight months. Oh, she sold the magazines and purses, but by then, she had decided that proprietorship was not for her. She needed to be free, as she had termed it—out in the world. He resigned himself to hear her latest scheme.

Dinner passed amicably with no mention of the topic on everyone's mind. After supper, Pagan approached Mallory in his study.

"Uncle Mal, I know what I want to do," she began in her usual forthright manner.

Mallory prepared himself for the worst, or so he thought. "Sit down, Pagan, and let's talk about this. First, why aren't you working today?"

"I'm not cut out to be a secretary, and that is where they were sending me, there and to work as a receptionist at the health club. I need more than sitting behind a desk all day. I need adventure."

"So, you've come up with a job that has adventure? And requires no training or education, I suppose."

Her face lit up. "Yes, that's the best part. I can start right now."

He braced himself. "All right. What is this wonder job?"

She sat forward and took a deep breath—preparing for the dramatic moment. "I want to be a detective, just like you."

He waited a moment before reacting. "A policeman? Pagan, I am a police officer."

She shook her head. "No, I don't want to be a policeman, just a detective. You are a police detective. I want to be a regular detective. Then, when I become established you can quit your job, and we can be partners. But we can work together before that. You can get leads from work and pass them on to me, and I can investigate. It will be great—perfect."

"But you have no training as a detective, and besides, the work is too dangerous. No, no. It's out of the question. Think up something else, sweetheart. Start a business or something. I'll lend you the money."

"I'll start taking shooting lessons, and practicing on people in the neighborhood. Not shooting at them—I mean spying on them. I'll be really good. What if I prove to you I can do the job, then will you help me?"

"No. Anyway, how would you prove it?"

"I could help you solve the *Rose* case."

He looked at the file lying on his desk. "Damn it, Pagan. Did you go through my files?"

"I just glanced at it. Boy, is it interesting. Do you have any leads?"

Closing his eyes in exasperation, he leaned back in his chair and began to count to ten. He made it all the way to three before she interrupted him.

"Don't be mad at me. I'm sorry, but I really can help. No one will expect me to be watching. I will blend into the woodwork."

He opened his eyes. "Has it ever occurred to you that this is dangerous work? It's not a game. Young women are being killed." He paused to shake his head. "And you could never blend into the woodwork. No, I can't allow it."

He knew as soon as he said it that it was a mistake—a red flag before the bull. Her face set into lines he knew too well, so he tried another tact. "Pagan. If something happened to you, I would never forgive myself. I'm asking you, please don't do this. There are hundreds of other things you could do. Choose something else."

She nodded her head and kissed him goodnight, but he knew the discussion was not over. He could only pray she didn't do anything too dangerous—anything that would get her killed.

The photos didn't do them justice—didn't capture their presence, their essence—their song. Could he? Could he bring to life that which he had so beautifully brought to death? They were beautiful, and he had made that beauty everlasting. They would never grow older, and the ravage of time would never etch its mark on their faces. He had saved them that. It was his gift to them—to the world.

CHAPTER 3

▼

The ride back to the crime scene was disturbing with memories too fresh to be painted with the gray shades of vagueness only time would bring. He couldn't get the picture of the two victims out of his mind—like his subconscious wanted to tell him something that he just couldn't quite bring to the surface. Maybe instead of trying to avoid the memories he should encourage them. He pulled over when he came to entrance of the Cummins ranch, where James Tucker worked as ranch foreman.

Mr. Tucker had called 911 just after 8:00 yesterday morning and signed an official statement later that afternoon. Wanting to interview Tucker personally was just one of Mallory's strategies for covering all the bases. The drive to the ranch house was long and winding, hiding any view of the homestead until the very last curve. Being situated well back from the main road maintained the valued privacy of Cummins family.

Tucker watched him park in the circular drive, heading him off as he neared the front door.

"Detective Mallory?"

"Yes. And you're Tucker. Am I late?"

Tucker smiled and stuck out his hand. "No, not at all. I just thought it might be better if we discussed this away from the main house. My office is right here. Would that be all right?"

"Certainly."

"Would you like something to drink? Coffee? Iced tea?"

"No, thank you," he answered, taking a seat in front of the oak desk dominating the small office. "I appreciate you taking the time to see me this morning. I

16   Red Red Rose

realize you have already given a statement, but sometimes details come to mind later that never find their way into a police report."

"Sure," Tucker said, taking a seat behind the desk. "What would you like to know?"

"Maybe we could start with how you came to be in the vicinity in the first place."

"Well, normally, I wouldn't have been there, we had a report of a few cows getting out and wandering along the highway the night before. What I usually do is send one of the hands to herd in the cattle and repair the break in the fence. But this time I took care of the repair myself because I wanted to check for tracks down the fence line. We've had a couple of episodes where the fence was damaged by something trying to get in rather than cows trying to get out."

"Did you find anything?"

"Yes, I found a set of tracks leading into the woods. Cat tracks—possibly bob cat—possibly panther, so I followed them. That's when I discovered the body."

"Did the tracks lead all the way to the body?"

"No. The tracks were parallel to the body. The body caught my attention because of the red. When I first spotted it, I thought it was blood and that I had a dead cow on my hands. Maybe one that had been killed by the cat I was tracking. I walked over for a closer look."

"Think back carefully. I want you to give me your first impressions." Mallory was scribbling furiously in his notebook. Tucker waited until he was finished before continuing.

"At first, I didn't believe it was real. It looked like something out of a movie set—something staged. I looked around, expecting someone with a camera to come out of the woods and yell at me for ruining the take."

"But you didn't see anyone?"

"No. No one was there, and no one left. If they had been leaving, I would have heard them tramping through the woods."

Mallory brought to mind his own first impression of the scene. "Did you notice any tracks around the body?"

Tucker passed his hand over his eyes, as if to shield himself from the memory. "No. I mean, I didn't notice. Once, I realized it was a body, I called 911."

"Have you remembered anything you didn't mention to the police?"

Tucker thought hard for a minute. "No. I don't remember anything."

Mallory thanked him and left. Not much to go on there, but he'd had to try. Next, he would revisit the scene. All his previous attention had been given to the body itself. This time he would pay more attention to the scene of the crime.

Pagan parked on the side of the road, pulling into the woods just far enough to make the car unobtrusive, and she hoped, inconspicuous. Keeping in mind she could be following the same path used by the killer, she walked slowly, taking time to look for any clue that might link the predator to this route or give any indication of his identity. She was also careful to keep a close lookout for snakes.

The first few feet were uneventful, but about twenty feet in, she noticed some dark spots across a few plant leaves that might have been blood. The find gave her an eerie feeling, and she looked around to assure herself she was still alone. About ten feet farther down the path she found evidence even more convincing—red rose petals. Stooping down for a closer look, she noted they were relatively fresh and just now beginning to curl around the edges. She marked the spot with a piece of white masking tape, as she had the other, and moved on.

She didn't see anything else until she came near the area where the body was found. At the edge of the clearing, where the trees thinned and the tall grass began, a sheet of white paper hung tenaciously to a low branch. As she came closer, she could see writing and knew this might be important. Careful not to touch the curling sheet, she tried to read what was written inside. What she saw chilled her to the bone despite the heat from the hot Texas sun. She read the note aloud to make sure she had not made a mistake.

> They're none who are so blind
> As those who will not see
> You passed up number two, my friends
> And picked up number three.

✴   ✴   ✴   ✴

Mallory left the comfortable safety of his car and entered the wooded area with reluctance, much as he had done on the previous day. He wasn't really sure what he was looking for or why he felt so compelled to return to the scene. Hadn't forensics just gone over the area with a fine-toothed comb? Did he think he would find anything they had overlooked? He ducked down to miss a hanging poison ivy vine and caught his coat on the thorns of wild roses. How ironic.

He saw nothing unusual on the way to the clearing. He would have been surprised if he had. Of all the ways to enter the clearing, the way he had chosen was perhaps the most visible. A few steps farther down the path brought him to the beginning of the police tape. From this point on, he was in danger of damaging any overlooked forensic evidence. He continued with care, looking for anything, which might have been missed.

When he came to the place where the body had lain, he stopped. Outlined by a few remaining rose petals, the space looked naked—debased somehow, as if removing the corpse had done it a personal injury. The crushed grass was black with the stain of the victim's blood. Nurtured or desecrated? He was about to examine the ground further when a nearby sound alerted him that he was not alone.

Wrapping his hand around the gun in his holster, he walked toward the sound. Five steps later, he heard another sound, more disturbing than the first. Alarmed by the weak cry, he lost no time in crossing the small open field to reach the source of the low whine. By the time he reached the other side his gun was out and in firing position. Ready to open fire, he was more than a little surprised to see his niece on the business end of his weapon. She had turned at his approach—as surprised to see him, as he was to see her.

"Pagan. What in the hell are you doing here? I almost shot you."

"He's been back, Uncle Mal. He's been back since yesterday."

Before he had time to react, she ran headlong into his arms, just as she had so many times as a child.

"What happened? Did you see him? Have you found something?"

She pointed to the branch. "He left a note—another poem. And I think I found some blood."

"Where?"

"Back there," she said, pointing back toward the way she had come.

He pulled out his cell phone. "Jamison—Mallory. I need a forensic team at the site where we discovered yesterday's body. There may be some new evidence. Have them enter the woods from the West off CR 3496."

After replacing the phone, he walked over to the hanging piece of paper. "You didn't touch anything, did you?"

"No, I was very careful." Her voice was quiet—subdued. The enormity of what she had found was beginning to sink in.

He read the note, but made no comment. "You said you thought you found some blood. Where was that?"

"On some leaves back the way I came. I marked the spot with some masking tape on the tree. I found something else, too—some rose petals. I marked that, too." They walked back to the marked trees.

Mallory was impressed despite his disapproval and spent the next few minutes looking for other pieces of evidence that might have been overlooked. "What are you doing out here? Didn't it ever occur to you that coming here might be dangerous or illegal?"

"Sorry, Uncle Mal. I just wanted to see the place—get a feel for it. I thought it might help in my investigation."

"Pagan, you don't have an investigation. This is police work, and you are interfering."

She was saved the rest of what he was going to say by the arrival of the forensic team. They did a careful sweep of the area from the site of the note back to where Pagan had first entered the woods.

Two hours later, Mallory arrived at the station. Theo met him at his office door. "You look worn out, and it's barely noon. Want to join me for a cup of coffee and a bite of lunch?"

"We discovered some new evidence," he said in way of an answer.

"Really?"

"Yeah, let's go somewhere. I need to get your ideas on a couple of things. Did they finish the autopsy report?"

"Got it in my briefcase."

"Good."

Pagan drove around for some time after leaving the scene of the crime. She had thought that being an investigator would be fun and exciting, not unsettling. She had expected to be thrilled at discovering new evidence. Instead, she felt dirty, as if the crime had in some way sullied her. Was this what being a detective was all about?

She stopped the car at a neighborhood park and got out. Children were everywhere—running, climbing, swinging—innocent—oblivious to everything beyond their small world.

"Can you help me?"

Pagan looked down at the little girl tugging on her pants. She resembled a tiny blonde cherub in her pink flowered dress and pink baby-doll shoes.

"I need a drink," she said, pointing to the water fountain. "Can't reach it."

"Sure, Sweetie. I'll give you a lift." The little girl drank noisily. "What's your name?"

"Amber. I'm this many." The girl held up three grubby fingers, then, ran back to the slide.

20   Red Red Rose

Pagan walked over to a wooden bench and sat down. The women lying in the morgue had once been three, too. They might have played at this very park—sliding down the slide—riding the merry-go-round—never dreaming that in a few short years it would all be gone. Never suspecting the horror awaiting them. What did it all mean? Her father's voice rang clearly through her thoughts.

"Life is not fair, Pagan. You wanting it to be will not make it so. You've got to accept that."

She remembered her answer, "So what? I'm just supposed to give up? Give in to my fate—not try to make it better?"

He had given her that look. The one he seemed to save for such occasions. The one that said just try to understand what I am saying to you. "Of course not. You never give up trying. That's what life is all about. Trying to improve yourself—your world. But you can't always win, that's all. And that's okay. You can't control destiny—you can only help shape it. That's all any of us can do. And it's enough. You'll see."

Mallory stabbed at his salad as if he needed to capture the leaves instead of just lifting them from the bowl. After a couple of minutes he gave up and picked up his knife. The liver and onions smelled heavenly, but his mind was not on the food. He ate mechanically, not really giving the cook his due.

"You're a thousand miles away aren't you?" asked Theo.

He smiled. "Not a thousand. Just about twenty-five."

"What has you so upset?"

"There was a note. The killer left another poem."

"That you missed the first time? But you already have a poem, don't you? Wasn't there one left in the clothing?"

"Yes. This is a new poem. Apparently, the killer went back to the scene. He may have still been there when we arrived—watching. The poem suggested that we've missed a body. There's another one out there—undiscovered."

"Oh, my god. Anything to indicate where?"

"No."

"I'm sorry to hear that. Yes, I can see where that would be disturbing."

"That and the fact that my niece found the evidence."

She took a moment to cut her steak before responding. "I don't understand. You took your niece with you?"

"No. She decided she wanted to be a detective and came on her own. I had no idea she would be there."

"No wonder you're distracted. How old is she?"

"Twenty-five."

"And she discovered the new evidence?"

"Yes, and some that forensics had missed the day before."

"Beginner's luck or is she a chip off the old block, maybe?"

The possibility gave him pause. "Too soon to say. You think I should encourage her?"

Theo smiled. "I don't think anything yet. Would it be possible for me to meet the young lady?"

"I was hoping you would ask. Maybe you can talk some sense into her."

"I'd be happy to talk with her," she assured him, her words remaining noncommittal.

CHAPTER 4

▼

Mallory and Theo arrived back at the precinct with the autopsy report still unopened. Jamison met them at the door.

"Chief Redford's waiting for you in his office, Detective."

"Thanks Sergeant." He turned to Theo. "I'd like you to sit in on this. We'll probably be covering some of the same ground you and I will be covering later."

"Sure."

Chief Redford's office was the last door on the left at the end of a narrow hall. Although the city had appropriated money only two years ago for a new building complete with wood paneling, the new structure was still short on needed space and lacked the warmth of a modern office facility. Mallory rapped lightly on the door and went in, followed closely by Ms. Van Zandt.

"Mallory, Van Zandt. Glad you're here, Theo. I'd like to hear your take on all this. So, Mallory, give me an update on your morning's work."

After he and Theo were seated, Mallory outlined the events of the morning beginning with his interview with Tucker and omitting most of Pagan's involvement in the day's later events. Redford listened without interruption until he had finished.

"So, the killer would have us believe there have been three murders and that we have an undiscovered body waiting for us somewhere. Do you believe that, Van Zandt?"

She shrugged. "I don't really have any reason not to."

"But why would he tell us? What gain would it be to the killer?"

"Maybe nothing. I don't think the note was about gain. I think it was more about order. He is following his own set of rules—his own sense of order. By dis-

- 22 -

covering the bodies out of order you have violated his system—fractured his creation."

"So, now what?"

"He must be very angry and frustrated."

Mallory turned to her. "So what are we looking at? Revenge?"

"No, not like you're talking about, anyway. His anger might bring us an extra victim, but not like the others."

"What do you mean?"

"This victim will not be part of his plan—his design. This would more likely be a random killing—a balm to his anger."

"And his plan? What will become of that?"

"He will make adjustments—do something to restore order."

Mallory shifted in his chair. "So, let's suppose you're right. Everything he is doing means something—to him. Each step he takes is part of his insane plan. How does this help us?"

"It makes him predictable."

"Makes sense. Any ideas on the second victim?"

Theo tilted her head. "Well, realizing his bent for order, I would take the time of death of the first victim and the third victim and divide by two. Then, I would take the same type of look at the locations."

Redford stood up. "Sounds like a plan, Mallory. What do you think?"

"Why not? We've little else to go on at this point. That and the autopsy reports should give us a start."

Pagan walked around the park for about an hour before choosing a course of action. In true detective fashion she decided to find out all she could about the first victim, Tandy Gerald. From the newspaper accounts, she knew Ms. Gerald had been born and grew up in a small community outside Tyler called Rolling Hills. The drive took about twenty minutes.

Like so many small towns around the country, the community was build around a railroad track. The track was laid, and then the town built up around it. On one side of the track there was the town hall, the post office, and the barbershop and on the other side was the general store, the drug store, and the school. Crossing town sounded like a dangerous thing to do and might have been, except that five years ago the train had stopped coming and the track had been removed. Now, there was just a long, straight line of dirt defining the center of the town.

Pagan studied each side of the town and decided the drug store was her best bet. Maybe it was the benches sitting out front or maybe it was the assortment of

24   Red Red Rose

toys, tools, and trinkets prominently displayed in the store window. Somehow she knew this was where she needed to start.

The old wooden door was solid and heavy with a bell that announced her entrance like a cowbell calling the hands to dinner. Her teeth jarred with the ear-splitting sound, unlike those of the cluster of ladies huddled around the pharmacy counter who couldn't be bothered for as much as a look-see. Pagan glanced around. Images of Jimmy Stewart soda jerking a sundae for Donna Reed flashed before her as she stared at the original wooden counter complete with all brass fixtures. Pagan turned to look at the group of waiting women.

"Excuse me."

A silver haired post millennium version of Aunt Bee turned to face her. "Well, hello honey. Did you need something?"

All the women seemed to stop their conversations at once and turned to hear what she had to say. She hesitated. Blurting it out that she wanted to investigate the dead girl suddenly seemed blunt and tactless. On the other hand, if anyone could answer her questions, she had a feeling these women could.

"Well, I am doing a story on the life of Tandy Gerald and wondered if anyone could help me with some background information." There, she had said it.

Having all the usual gossipy attributes of a small town, Pagan didn't have to push hard to gather facts about the girl's life. A working mother and alcoholic father might have contributed to the girl's tendency toward a life of late night partying and easy relationships, but everyone agreed it surely hadn't caused it.

Tandy Gerald was pretty—no one could dispute that. And she hadn't deserved to die like that, but she was the type to get into trouble. Mary Fagan remembered when Tandy had run off for the weekend with the Miller boy and scared her parents half to death. And wasn't it not too long after that she had gone up North for the summer to visit her sick aunt. Gladys Freeman was sure it was, but Nelda Hastings thought it might have been the following summer. Of course, nothing ever came of it—her stint with the Miller boy. He went on to college, married Beatrice Ledbetter, and moved farther down South—hell and gone from Rolling Hills. After two hours, Pagan had an interesting picture of the life and times of Tandy Gerald and a great-sounding recipe for cherry cheesecake, but was no closer to the girl's killer or the reason for her death.

As the name of the second victim had not been released, she decided to try another tact. She already had a vital piece of information about the killer. He had some interesting ideas about the use of roses. Where better to perpetrate his crimes? Didn't Tyler tout itself as being the Rose Capital of the World? Maybe he was a rose grower? Or possibly the dissatisfied employee of a rose grower? Was his use of the flower intended as an honor or an indignity? Somehow she felt it was an honor—a reverence.

The roses splashed vibrant color against the cerulean blue of the clear Texas sky. She had loved her roses. Bought them in bags and soaked them for about an hour before planting. While they were soaking, she dug holes in the garden and set up tiny tags to label the rose bushes according to their specific variety. Vine roses were planted in the back of the garden along the trellises—trellises she hand painted year after year with white paint. They splayed straight and tall toward heaven—her connection to God—to immortality. Summer heat released the sweet perfume, tinting the air with the pungent scent. Evenings in the garden were special times. Their time—a time of stories and magic. She'd held him in her arms, and they'd laughed. The love they shared was pure and good. She would never have left him of her own free will. Never.

Mallory's office was clean and functional. Above and beyond that, the most that could be said was that it had a window—which was saying quite a lot. Many of the offices in the building had only internal walls, dooming their occupants to reside under the stark glow of fluorescent luminescence. The floor space was scant with an old pine desk being the most prominent feature—scuffed a bit, but large. Ample space for all the neat piles of folders which defined his organizational skills and ordered his life. When he and Theo entered the room, their minds were not on office decor but on two girls lying cold and stiff in the hospital morgue.

"I suggest we begin with a list of knowns. Do you have the medical file on Gerald?"

Theo reached into her bag, bringing the autopsy report to one of the few clean spaces atop the desk.

Mallory picked up the phone, fingers pressing the squared numbers almost without thought. "Gail, Mallory here. Have you received the report on the second victim? Good. Would you bring it down, please? Thanks. Also, I'd like you and Jamison to meet me for a few minutes in my office."

He took the photographs of the two girls and pinned them to the wall, as if he were about to present a lecture. The shots included photos taken before their deaths as well as the death scenes themselves. Mallory couldn't help but wonder how many other photos would find their way to the wall before the killer was apprehended. A knock on the door let him know Whiting and Jamison had arrived. Greetings were exchanged and dismissed. Gail took the remaining chair and Jimmy Jamison leaned against a corner table.

26   Red Red Rose

"Did you bring the report?"

"Yes," Gail said, opening the folder.

"Have you read it?"

"Yes."

"Good. Just hang on to it for a few minutes. First, let's hear the report on Gerald. Theo, would you like to give us a run-down on the Gerald autopsy?"

She lifted the report from the desk. "Tandy Gerald was a twenty-two year old woman. Caucasian—five-foot seven—one hundred and twenty-seven pounds. She died on the morning of July 12th between 5:00 a.m. and 6:00 a.m. Cause of death—exsanguination—loss of blood. The carotid artery had been severed. The victim also sustained a head wound as well as superficial cuts shaped like the letter 'A' to the chest and abdomen. There was no evidence of sexual trauma."

"Were there any defensive wounds?"

"No, according to the report, Gerald was unconscious when the killer used the knife."

"Stomach contents?"

"Rice, sautéed vegetables, and MSG."

"Chinese food. Okay, thanks, Theo. Any questions or comments?"

"Where was the head wound? Front or back of the head?" asked Jamison, leaning forward.

"Back."

"Then, can we assume she knew her assailant?"

Gail turned in her seat. "No, I don't think so. He could have hit her from behind without her ever seeing him."

"But how did he know the blow would render her unconscious?"

"He probably didn't."

"Wasn't that kind of risky?"

Theo spoke up. "Maybe that was part of the thrill. Anyway the wound doesn't rule out a backup plan, and we don't know that he didn't have one in place. However, the blow was hard enough to have caused permanent injury—crushing the skull. I feel sure he had very little fear of the woman regaining consciousness."

"Thank you. Let's move on to the second victim. Whiting, would you brief us on that?"

"Her name was Nancy Starnes. Caucasian—twenty-five years old—five-foot-five—one hundred and twenty pounds. Died on the morning of July 18th between 5:30 a.m. and 7:00 a.m. from a crushing blow to the back of the skull resulting in a hemorrhage of the posterior cerebral cortex. Her carotid artery was cut and she had superficial cuts over her abdomen and chest, also in the shape of the letter 'A.' According to the report, she was dead when the artery was cut."

"So, basically our killer tried to commit two identical murders—only he hit the second one a little too hard. Did it matter to him that the head wound killed Starnes instead of her bleeding to death? Theo?"

"I doubt it. Not as long as the blood continued to flow. If, on the other hand, the blow to the head had caused her to die instantly instead of some time later, the heart wouldn't have continued to pump out her blood. I think that would have mattered to him. The blood seems to be the key. Could I take a look at the poems?"

"Sure." Mallory flipped through the file, producing the two poems.

Theo studied them for a minute. "Okay here. Listen to this:

> Seeping her into the soil
> Nourishing the earth
>
> I bleed.
> You bleed.
> We all bleed.
> Ring around the rosy.
> I, too, will feed the earth she loved.
> Drip blood upon the rose.

These lines from the first poem refer directly to the blood and how the blood is nourishing the earth. It's as if the murders are sacrifices to some kind of sacred belief. He is feeding the earth with the blood of the victims. I don't think the death is what is important here. The blood is."

Jamison spoke from the back. "Then, our killer sees himself as some sort of priest or maybe avenger. If soaking the earth with blood is a holy act to him then the more blood—the holier he becomes. The entire process becomes a mission to him—a crusade."

"Yes," Gail added, "I think you're right, but there is another element as well. The poem used the word, 'she.' What was it? Will you read that line again, Theo?"

> "I, too, will feed the earth she loved.
> Drip blood upon the rose."

"Don't you see? The victims are the sacrifice—the blood goes to nourish the earth—but the key is the love he felt for this woman. He is doing it for her."

Jamison nodded. "So, the woman he loved is gone. Did she die and this brought on the murders? Do we read the obits for the recent death of a woman?"

Theo shook her head. "No. Action doesn't usually fall within the scope of grief unless revenge is involved. I would think this is an old grief, reactivated by a recent event acting as a catalyst."

Mallory pinned the poems on the wall beside the pictures. "So, what does this all mean? And what about the 'A?' Any ideas? Are we back to square one?"

"No," Theo answered. "We don't have all the answers, but I think we have gone a long way to establish motive. I think opportunity has to fall into place next. Where and when were the girls taken? Was this man dating them? How were they selected? Do they have anything in common?"

"Good. Whiting—Jamison. See what you can find out on that. Meanwhile, I think you should be aware there has been another note. Yesterday, when I returned to the scene, I found a piece of paper with a short verse.

> They're none who are so blind
> As those who will not see
> You passed up number two, my friends
> And picked up number three."

Gail was the first to react. "There is another body out there?"

"If we can believe the killer, there is."

"But why would he tell us—help us along?" asked Jamison.

Everyone looked to Theo. "Well, I think we may have offended his sense of order for one thing. Also, he refers to us as 'my friends' like we're somehow in this together—working on the same side."

"Why would he think that?"

"Why wouldn't he? If he is the priest—on a mission—doing what is right and holy and we are the defenders of justice, then to him, we are on the same side."

CHAPTER 5

▼

Pagan pulled her car into the driveway. The time was almost six o'clock, and she knew Maria would have dinner ready. She also knew Maria would be expecting her to eat. She had been a regular guest since Uncle Mal had moved to East Texas about nine months ago. He had suggested more than once she give up her travel-trailer, store it, and make this her home. The house was large, and the guest bedroom would give her all the privacy she needed. So, why hadn't she moved in? Well, at first, it just seemed to be an imposition. And then, well…. She wasn't really sure. Of course, that was before she had decided to become a detective. Now, it would make perfect sense for her to move in. She might even bring it up at dinner tonight.

Maria met her at the door. "Ah, Pagan. You uncle is late. Could you do me a quick favor?"

"Sure, Maria. What do you need?"

"Rolls. The cat got into the house again and headed straight for my dinner rolls. That cat is evil. And no snakes. He has not caught one," she finished, wagging her finger threateningly toward the back door.

"I'd be happy to go for you, Maria. Won't take but a few minutes."

She slid back behind the wheel of the small car and headed toward the nearest convenience store. Uncle Mal lived in a nice section of town. The large brick homes were older—the original owners having seen their kids through high school and moved on. What this meant was that while the houses had settled on their foundations, the landscape had grown up. Transplanted trees in pots were now towering oaks overhanging the street. The effect was beautiful—a quiet peaceful place to live.

The nearest store was five blocks away—a magnet for local kids in search of an after-school snack. The parking lot was filled with vehicles, but the Ghia could fit in places most small cars couldn't. She squeezed out of the door without managing to chip the car next to her, but barely. She held little hope the passenger in the next car would show her the same courtesy.

Locating the rolls was easy. She was on her way to one of the front lines to pay, when a familiar voice stopped her.

"Well, hello again."

She turned to the sound of the voice. The face of the attractive-looking man in the pullover cardigan and Dockers was that of a stranger, but the voice was one she had heard recently. Was she supposed to know this man? Had she gone to school with him? Worked with him? She smiled and tried to mimic a look of recognition.

"Hello. Doing a little late night shopping?"

"You don't remember me, do you?"

"Sort of. Your voice sounds familiar. Have we met?"

"Not formally. My name is Chad DeForest." He paused expectantly.

"Mine is Pagan Mallory. Now that we are through the introductions, where did we not formally meet?"

His smile was contagious. "At another convenience store. I was wearing a rather large hat and you were searching for your sunglasses?"

She gave him a long assessing look. "Well, aren't you a diverse fellow? So, which are you—the preppie or the cowboy? Or are you something else entirely?"

"What would I have to be to get your phone number, Pagan Mallory?"

She smiled. "I'll tell you what. You can give me yours."

"Will you call me?"

Her smile broadened. "I might."

Dinner was pleasant. Maria had cooked a pot roast with potatoes and carrots. Both Pagan and Mallory worked hard to do justice to the splendid meal. Maria beamed. Cooking, to her, was the supreme act of love. She could have happily made food for an entire house-full of people. Dessert was Sweet Potato Pie—Mallory's favorite. After supper, he closeted himself in his office while Pagan helped Maria clean up the kitchen. After the dishes were finished, Pagan prepared a tray with two cups of coffee and knocked on her uncle's door.

"Uncle Mal, can I talk to you a minute?"

"And she comes bearing coffee? This must be important."

Pagan gave him his coffee and took hers to the orange leather chair. "Well, I was wondering if your offer of room and board still stood? I seem to spend most of my time here anyway."

"We'd love to have you here. No sense living in that mobile when we have this place. When were you thinking of moving in?"

Pagan took a sip of her coffee. "I was thinking about this weekend, if that's all right."

"Sounds great. Do you need any help packing or loading?"

"Nah, don't have that much stuff. I travel light."

"Okay, then it's settled." He studied her closely. "What else you got on your mind?"

She smiled. "How can you always tell? I've got something I'd like you to look at."

"Have you been painting again?"

"No, nothing like that. I did some background research on Tandy Gerald today, and I wanted you to read my notes. I thought you might find it helpful. And before you start with the lectures, it wasn't dangerous, and it didn't interfere with anything."

The slight lift of his eyebrows was Mallory's only reaction. "I'll read them as long as you realize that my agreeing to read them doesn't mean I approve. All right?"

"I understand. Thanks, Uncle Mal."

Theodora Van Zandt watched her Siamese cat pace back and forth along the back of the couch.

"No, Pi. You're not going out tonight. Last time I let you out for the evening you didn't come home for three days. Friday, I'll take you to Dr. Stephen's, and he'll make you feel all better. Now, come on down here and play with Opie. Look at how lonely he is all by himself."

Theo looked at the opossum curled at her feet. She hadn't really intended to have an opossum as a pet. One day it had just happened. She had been out walking in the country when she had discovered the abandoned baby opossum. His leg was broken. Without giving the matter a lot of thought, she had bundled him up in her sweater and taken him straight to her vet. The doctor was reluctant to treat the wild animal, but Theo was insistent, and Opie became an official member of the family. That was six months ago.

Piwacket wasn't much more than a baby himself then and they became immediate friends—well, that is as immediate as a Siamese cat becomes a friend with anyone. Now, they slept and ate together, and Opie used the cat box just like Pi did. What Opie didn't do was jump on everything in the house. He was a climber. If the object was climbable then, Opie would find his way right to the top.

Theo had lived in the same two-story brick house for the last twenty-five years. She and her husband bought the house right after they married. When he died eight years ago, she had stayed, even though the house was much too large for just one person. For a time, she ran her practice out of the house. Now, she just kept it for her own comfort and enjoyment—and that of her cat's, of course.

Having the extra room gave her the space to indulge in some of her favorite things—like her Christmas tree room. She loved Christmas and had an entire room devoted to it. Garlands of holly outlined a room illuminated by festively decorated trees covered in hundreds of tiny bright lights. Miniature towns of snow topped buildings and gift-filled houses covered tables of glittered white to add to the holiday atmosphere, creating a fantasy world in the magic room of make-believe. At anytime during the year she could step into her private sanctuary and enjoy Christmas.

Theo needed her retreats to heal her from the harsh realities of life she dealt with on a daily basis. She opened her briefcase and removed the file of what was beginning to be referred to as the "Rose" murders. She studied the two photographs she had of the two victims and reread the poems. To the killer, this was clearly an act of love. Piwacket jumped into her lap for some attention. She stroked his head absently as she tried to get into the head of the killer. An act of love that was also an act of grief carried to its most extreme enactment.

The phone rang interrupting her thoughts. Mallory's voice on the other end of the line carried finality as well as a broad hint of frustration. "I just got a call that the second body has been found. I…I thought you would like to know."

"You're on your way to the scene?"

"Yes."

"I'd like to be there. Would you mind if I showed up?"

"You're not far from me. Why don't I give you a lift?"

"Thanks, I'd appreciate that."

Pagan was awakened by the late night ringing of the telephone. She had fallen asleep on the couch watching a rerun of one of her favorite movies, *Last of the Dogmen.* Hitting the mute button, she slipped the receiver to her ear the moment it stopped ringing. A call this late had to be important.

"Hello." Her uncle's voice sounded groggy with unfulfilled sleep.

"Mallory—Redford. We've located another body. Are you familiar with the overpass on the North side?"

"Over the railroad? Yeah, sure."

"Well, there is a red freight storage building on the South side of the tracks. The body is located in a ditch behind the building."

"I'm on my way."

"Good. I've called forensics. You might give Van Zandt a call. We could use her impressions."

Pagan feigned sleep until she heard her uncle start the car. After his lights cleared the drive, she made a beeline to her own car. This was her chance to get in on the ground floor—to see the scene of the crime first hand. The thought of getting caught or what her uncle might say never really crossed her mind. Throwing the car into gear, she reached for her half empty bottle of Diet Coke and took a long swig. That helped, but she longed for a cup of coffee.

Getting across town was easy. Not much traffic at three o'clock in the morning. However, sneaking up on a crime scene in a bright yellow Karmann Ghia was a bit tricky. There were people everywhere. What could she say to explain her presence? A list of possibilities ran through her mind—all of which she rejected. Keep it simple. Wasn't that what everyone always said? All right. She would say her uncle had asked her to take notes and try to stick to the shadows. If she was lucky, she might be finished by the time her uncle arrived.

The area under the overpass was well lit, but the red storage building was dark—the yard behind it even darker. Police cars were parked with their lights on, aimed toward a central point. She turned off her headlights as she neared the scene and parked a building away. From there she approached with stealth, like a wolf inching his way toward the warmth of a Boy Scout campfire. In the frenzy of activity, she was practically invisible.

She walked toward the dark shape in the ditch, where the light didn't quite reach. Officers were shining their flashlights—trying to get a better look at the rose covered corpse. The lines of narrow light didn't do the scene justice, like looking at a picture through a mask of circular holes. The limited sight only increased everyone's curiosity, making it more intense. They moved steadily closer, shrinking the circle between themselves and the victim.

She moved in too, drawn to the circle despite the danger of being seen—despite the horror awaiting her there. For what had started out for the killer as a scene of beauty had been destroyed. The pretty red rose petals had darkened, withered—blown away in places to reveal the rotting corpse underneath. Nothing could remain untainted for long under the torrid breath of the harsh Texas

34   Red Red Rose

sun. As the group moved nearer to the ditch, the air was still—holding in the putrid stench until they were close and then releasing it suddenly, like one last dying breath.

Pagan gasped, doubling over in an involuntary reaction she was powerless to hide or stop. Knees in the dirt with both hands clasped to her mouth, she fought for control. The circle moved forward without her? What were these men made of? She was distracted by the lights of another car driving onto the scene. Unable to see past the glare of the headlights she could only suspect that the sounds of two doors opening and closing were made by her uncle and Theo Van Zandt. In a few seconds her suspicions were confirmed when the pair walked in front of the headlights and onto the scene. Chief Redford disengaged himself from the group of men circling the corpse and walked out to meet him.

"Mallory. Van Zandt," Redford greeted them as the distance closed.

"Is this the body of the second victim?"

"Appears so. I'm afraid this corpse is in much worse shape than either of the other two bodies. Of course, the killer's note prepared us for that."

"Has the forensic team done a sweep yet?"

"They arrived a few minutes ago, but had to send out for a Bell light. The area was too dark to collect evidence. Come on down. The team is making do with flashlights."

Pagan stayed where she was, low and in the shadows, as her uncle walked in her direction. Accepting a light from one of the team, he took a long look at the body. "Did you find her clothes?"

Redford answered him. "Yes. The clothes and the poem."

Mallory stepped away from the body. "Could I see it?"

Redford walked to his car and removed a plastic bag. The note was inside.

> The earth's a womb that holds the dead
> "Redrum, Redrum" the shiny man said.
> Umbilical cord, I hold the string
> Summer, fall, winter, spring.
>
> Love me tender, love me do
> Roses for me and death to you
> I'll cut your neck, you'll give your all
> Winter, spring, summer, fall

Jack be nimble Jack be slow
Watch my numbers start to grow.
Soon you'll know that it is real
Spring, summer, winter, kill.

*   *   *   *

Mallory read the poem twice before handing the evidence bag back to Redford. "I'd like a copy when forensics is through, although I don't expect them to find anything."

"Did you gleam any new information from that one?"

He thought for a minute. "The mother image comes through in this one. Could be something. Could be nothing or worse—a false lead."

Both men turned at the approach of a large truck. "That must be the Bell light. Want to take a look after it's hooked up? Maybe the new perspective will provide us with some added information." Redford replaced the note and the men started back down the hill to where the Bell light was being set up.

CHAPTER 6

▼

Pagan watched them from her vantage point, inching her way toward the police car and the plastic bag containing the note. How she was going to manage to extract the note from the car without detection was a puzzle. But she felt confident she would think of something.

The Bell light was large and heavy—if the groans from the men lifting it were any indication. For the space of about fifteen seconds, every eye in the immediate vicinity was turned toward the light. This was her chance—perhaps her only chance to read the note. Once the poem left this site she had little hope of ever seeing it again. The only way she even knew about the poems was by snooping through the file on her uncle's desk, and he probably wouldn't allow that to happen again.

Now to get to the note. Opening the car door would turn on the inside light and attract attention. Not an option. She stared at the car. The window on the passenger side was cracked open about four inches. If she stretched out her arm and her fingers, she just might be able to reach the plastic bag on the dash. It was her only chance. With a quick look round to reassure herself that she wasn't being watched, she slipped her arm through the window. Pushing toward the dash, she wiggled her fingers in hopes of touching the bag. Nothing. She felt the hard surface of the dash, but no plastic. She removed her arm and looked again. Her fingers had to have been close.

Trying again, she moved her arm farther toward the front of the car. This, although very uncomfortable, should give her the extra length she needed to reach the note. In a few seconds of exquisite torture she knew she had been right. She had the note. Stepping away from the car, she pulled a penlight from her pocket and quickly scanned the poem. Eerie, just like the others. Reading it again more slowly, she tried to commit what she could to memory. Now to get to a pen and paper. Without touching the note, she sealed the bag and was about to return it to the car, when a strong hand clasped her around the elbow. She started, her heart tried to jump through her chest, and the bones in her legs suddenly felt like cheap rubber.

"What the hell do you think you're doing?" a deep voice demanded, only inches from her ear.

She wanted to respond, to say something witty and clever—something to distract him from her real purpose. Her throat felt as if it were closing, her mouth full of cotton. She looked toward the voice. His face was in the shadows, as was hers. Probably a beat cop pulling this assignment as some sort of punishment. Just a guard. Obviously, not one of the inner circle—not familiar with the faces of the men and women in the detective division or their outside experts. Sure, why not go for it? She croaked out the first thing that popped into her mind. "Let go of my arm. Who are you to question me? I'm here on official business, and unless you wish to be cited for obstruction, I suggest you go back to your post." There—it was out. Now, to see if it worked.

"Mind if I take a look at your badge?"

"Mind if I see yours?"

She could imagine him smiling at her in the darkness, knowing she was bluffing. He flashed something in front of her that looked official. She gave it a cursory glance without bothering to read, rapidly planning her next move.

"Now, it's your turn."

"I don't carry a badge," she replied, using her most intimidating tone. "I am a criminal profiler on special assignment. Now, if you don't mind—it's late, and I have a lot of work to do."

"Sorry to have bothered you, Ms. I don't believe I caught your name."

"Quite all right. You were just doing your job. And as we're not likely to cross paths again, I find the exchange of our names to be pointless. Don't you?" Tucking the note under her arm, she walked away, hoping the stranger would follow her example. When she had gone far enough to feel safe, she risked a look back. He was gone. Relief washed over her with the suddenness of a spring shower. Moving as quickly as possible without attracting attention, she returned the note to the Chief's car and headed for the Ghia. Never had the little car looked so good.

She turned the key and found the road without benefit of her lights, thankful an unexpected pothole had not swallowed her up. About a hundred feet from where she had parked, she risked illumination. Yes. She had done it. Excitement coursed through her like a good wine. She had penetrated a crime scene, conducted an investigation under the noses of the veteran detectives, and no one was the wiser. What could be better than this? She pulled off the main road absorbed in her thoughts, unaware of the narrowed pair of eyes patiently watching her exit.

Mallory woke up early the following morning despite his crime scene activities the night before. Debating on whether or not to get up, he let the smell of Maria's coffee help him cast the deciding vote. By the time he reached the kitchen, scrambled eggs were waiting on the table along with a generous amount of bacon and brown gravy. The only thing missing was the smell of biscuits baking in the oven.

"Is this a holiday? What happened to fussing about my diet?"

Maria clucked her tongue. "When you have no sleep, you must eat extra food to make up for it. I heard you leave the house in the middle of the night, then you get up early this morning for more work. So, I make you special breakfast to give you strength."

"Looks great, Maria, but you have enough food here for two or three breakfasts."

"Pagan will be down soon. She needs food, too. Nobody sleeps anymore."

Mallory frowned at the implication. What did Maria know that he didn't? Maybe Pagan had gone out on a date last night. He must remember to ask her.

Maria joined him at the table. "They discovered the missing body. Yes?"

"Yes."

"Was it covered in the roses like the others?"

Mallory took a bite of his eggs and chewed, his mind returning to the night before. "Same as the others, covered in petals. So far we have managed to keep the reporters at bay, but when this hits the news, all hell is going to break loose in this city."

"Ah, you must catch him. You will. Killers make mistakes. You always get them."

Mallory's look became thoughtful. "Sounds so simple when you say it. I only wish it were true. Truth is we don't catch them all. Some we leave to God, not by choice. Oh, by the way, I've invited a guest for dinner tonight."

Maria's eyes lit up. "You invite that nice woman helping the police? Will be good to meet her."

"No. I've invited a visiting FBI agent who is assisting me on the case. I guess I could ask her to join us. And ask Pagan when she gets up. I know she'll want to be here to pick up any tidbits of information that might be dropped."

"I thought you didn't want Pagan involved in the case."

"I don't, but you know Pagan. She is already involved. This way I can, at least, keep an eye on her."

Her expression became hooded. "So, she won't be sneaking out on her own."

"Exactly."

Pagan, too, woke to the smell of Maria's coffee—only not quite so early as her uncle. The minute her eyes opened she thought of the case and what she would do today to solve it. What could she do? Well, she could conduct interviews like she had yesterday. Never could tell when something important would crop up. She thought back to last night's adventure. The entire experience had taken on dream-like qualities in the stark light of day. In this dream—she had taken on the police force and won. She was a sleuth—a spy—an undercover agent for truth, justice, and the American way. For a few minutes she just sat there, hugging her knees to her chest—reliving the whole glorious experience.

Today she would find out about Nancy Starnes—where she had lived, worked, hung out. When she found out everything, she would compare the two girls—find out what they had in common. By then, she might know the name of the third girl. Which reminded her of her second plan. Her meeting with the man last night had given her the idea. She would locate someone in the department—not too bright, but smart enough to gather information and use him to find out about the case. Surely, there was someone she could use. Not unattractive, she was sure she could locate some lonely policeman who would be very pleased to share secrets with her. Her day planned out—she dressed and headed downstairs for breakfast and the taste of Maria's wonderful coffee.

Janet Stevimeyer studied the bottles of nail polish lined up on the tiny wall shelf. Her favorite color, hands down, was "No, I'm Not Really a Waitress" red. However, true red in the middle of summer could make a girl look cheap and easily attainable. Better try something else for a while. Maybe purple or green. She looked around. Paul, the Vietnamese nail stylist who sculptured her nails was growing impatient. She'd ask him about the color. Picking up the two bottles, she made her way back to the small table and sat down.

"You choose purple or green?" he asked, eyeing the two bottles.

"I don't know. What do you think?"

40   Red Red Rose

Paul held both against her skin. "Purple. Green not good."

In ten more minutes, she was finished and on her way out. She didn't usually get her nails done during the week, but tonight she had a special reason—a date. Not that she didn't have dates on a regular basis, but guys she picked up in bars really didn't count. Just a little too smooth for her taste—oily smooth. Quick with the lines, the moves, and the two dollar shots that kept a girl off center until they could move in for the kill. Once that was done, it was just a matter of bag 'um and tag 'um. Which in her experience meant rifle through her purse and then, dump her at the first possible moment.

But this guy was different. First of all, she hadn't picked him up in a bar. Second, he seemed like a genuinely nice guy. She had met him in the plant section of Go Mart and thought he was gay. Not that she had anything against gays, some of her good friends were gay. She had found, however, they made lousy bisexual partners, even when she bought the shots.

"I can't help but notice you seem to be having trouble selecting a root stimulator. Perhaps I might make a suggestion." That was how he had opened the conversation. When she nodded, he picked one of the bottles from the shelf, placing it into her buggy. By that time, she'd had a good chance to check him out. Not exactly handsome, but interesting—intelligent. Casual clothes—expensive— wore the money easily as if he were used to it or unimpressed by it.

When he invited her out for a coffee, she readily accepted. The experience was pleasant enough. She talked about her childhood, her job—her hobbies. In fact, come to think of it, she had really talked a lot. He knew everything about her, and she knew almost nothing about him, except that he was a good listener. But some men liked that—talkative women. After all, he had invited her out again. Gosh, what time was it? She still had to pick out a new dress. Something smart. Something he would like. Something to die for.

Pagan looked at the numbers painted on the mailbox. Yes, this was the place, but could she really do it? What choice did she have if she wanted to be a real detective? This was what investigators did. They investigated. All right, get a grip. How hard could it be? She checked her bag for the tenth time to assure herself that her notebook was inside. Then, she opened the car door and got out.

The house was a combination of frame and brick, firmly middle class. God, there was a wreath on the door. She'd never get through this without barfing. She was just about to leave when the door suddenly opened.

"Yes, may I help you?"

"Mrs. Starnes? My name is Pagan Mallory, and I'm investigating the death of your daughter, Nancy. Could I have a few minutes of your time?"

The silver-headed woman stepped aside, allowing her to pass into the room. Pagan went inside, feeling like an intruder—that she was violating something sacred. But she wasn't, was she? She was one of the good guys. What she was doing wasn't wrong, was it? She didn't want to intrude on the mother's grief—pry memories from her—force her to share the only thing she had left of her child. God, she felt sick.

"Won't you sit down, Ms. Mallory?"

"Please, call me Pagan."

"Okay, Pagan. How can I help you?"

The irony of the woman's question struck her with the force of a blow. She answered her as honestly as she could. "I want to help you, Mrs. Starnes. I want to find the man who took your daughter's life and stop him. You can help me by sharing information about your daughter. Can you do that, Mrs. Starnes? If it's too painful, I understand, and I'll leave."

The woman bowed her head, and even though she didn't make any noise, Pagan knew she was crying. She put her notebook back into her bag and closed it, blinking away tears of her own. She was almost to the door when the woman stood to her feet.

"No, wait. Please. I'd like to help you. I want you to know my daughter."

CHAPTER 7

▼

Mrs. Starnes stood up, and Pagan followed her up the stairs. "I didn't realize that Nancy had still lived at home."

Without answering, Mrs. Starnes walked up the last of the stairs and opened the door to Nancy's room. "She didn't. But we kept it for her so she could spend the occasional night or weekend here. She lived with a roommate in an apartment complex off Old Jacksonville Highway, The Southern Pines. Been there about two years. That way she could be more independent—have more privacy. Not that her father and I intruded on her life. But I'm rambling. Let's go in."

Pagan followed her into the room, totally unprepared for what she would find there. The walls of the room were pale turquoise, covered in hand-painted scenes. The artwork was arresting. She walked over for a closer look. Rich in detail, the pictures overlapped each other like a collage, but stood out independently as well.

The theme was a giant wood. Aged trees, gnarled and knotted, stretched their branches over the walls and ceiling of the bedroom, their mottled green leaves moving gently in a slow wind. Summer shadows fell across small animals and birds nestled in the limbs and played on the ground below. The mood was quiet and peaceful—a nice nature picture, if the artist had stopped with that. She hadn't. Peeking throughout the scene were faces—human faces—noticeable, without being distracting. Some hung in the open air while others emerged throughout the scene as part of the landscape, appearing and disappearing as the viewer's perspective shifted and grew. The effect was mesmerizing.

"Interesting, isn't it?"

Mrs. Starnes polite voice intruded on her thoughts, tearing her away from a world she wasn't prepared to leave.

"Interesting?" Pagan turned to look at the mother of the artist, wondering if she had any idea of how special her daughter had been. "Mrs. Starnes, this is wonderful. Your daughter had a tremendous talent. Do you have any of her other work?"

Mrs. Starnes sat down on the gold chenille bedspread. "There isn't any other work. This is it. She would add to it from time to time, but never started anything else. She said it was her life."

Pagan looked back at the wall. "Do you recognize any of these people?"

"Sure. They were people she knew."

Pagan looked more closely. What if she had known him? What if Nancy and the killer had been friends or lovers? What if he was here—immortal—on Nancy's forest wall? The thought gave her an eerie feeling, as if she was being watched.

"How long ago did she start the wall? Do you remember?"

For a minute the woman didn't answer, just stared, lost in her memories. When she finally did speak, her voice was strained. "She was sixteen. I remember because we had just celebrated her birthday. Balloons, streamers, big cake, the whole bit. All her friends were there. Janie and Debbie from school and, of course, Wayne, the guy she was dating. I don't remember all their names. She had a lot of friends. The party lasted late—into the early morning. After everyone had gone, she came up here. I thought she was asleep and wouldn't have come in, but I saw the light under her door."

Mrs. Starnes stopped the story. She stood up and walked over to the wall, placing her hand on one of the faces. "Here," she said, lightly touching the edge of the drawing. "Nancy started the painting here, with this face. When I asked her what she was doing, she said she was painting her life on the wall so she would remember it. Like a picture diary."

"When was the last time she painted on the wall?"

"The weekend before she died."

Pagan turned back to look once more at the wall. The eyes on the faces stared down, willing her to study them—willing her to uncover their secret—Nancy's secret—as if their painted mouths were whispering and only she could hear.

The autopsy report read like the plot line of a cheap novel—trite—predictable. Mallory gave it a cursory glance before handing it back to Theo. "Not much on varying the MO is he? As certain as a rainy wedding day in April."

Theo reread the report. "Okay, we know what is the same. Let's see what is not."

44   Red Red Rose

"What do you mean?"

"I mean let's look all the tiny variables and see if they can tell us anything."

"All right, like what?"

"Here, let me get a pen and paper, and we'll make a list."

Mallory watched her exit through the swinging door, then took a moment to inventory the large kitchen. When Theo had suggested going to her house for lunch, he hadn't been too keen on the idea. Surely a public place would be more suitable to discuss the case. Going to a house seemed a little too friendly. Or was it just that he had an aversion to sandwiches? Anyway, after two bowls of Theo's homemade soup, he was convinced he had been wrong.

The kitchen was bright—cheerful, and the eating nook was bordered by windows on two sides—giving an open feeling to the entire area. Two glass door cabinets flanked the entrance to the dining nook, backing up into the kitchen. There, she had stored a variety of whatnots and topped them with two ivy plants. The effect was cozy, but uncluttered. Acknowledging that he couldn't eat another bite, Mallory began to clear the table. By the time Theo returned, the dishes were all put away.

"Sorry, to be so long. Took a phone call from the office. The name of the third victim is Carla Clumb." She stopped when she saw the table. "Oh, how nice. You've cleared everything away. Here is the pen and paper."

"Carla Clumb."

"Yes, does the name ring a bell?"

"No. Have they finished the autopsy report?"

"Not yet," she said, joining him at the table. "Are you ready to start on our list? I thought we might begin with location. I brought a map." After spreading the map across the table, they marked the points where the bodies had been discovered.

"Do you think it's random?"

"No, I don't believe it is, but I'll be damned if I can see a pattern to it. What else?"

"We need to know if they knew each other or had a common acquaintance. What about their jobs? Where did they go to school?"

"We should have all that information in the next couple of days. Jamison and Whiting are looking into it."

"We have a volunteer helping out on some of the lighter detective work. My niece, Pagan. She has already done some background on the first victim."

"Good. What is our next step?"

"I want to know more about the roses. He has to be getting them from somewhere."

Pagan could scarcely wait to reach her Uncle's house. This new information could really be important. He would have to approve of her new profession now. When she got to the house, Maria was in a state of frenzy.

"I will never be finished in time. Everything must be perfect. The man is in the FBI, you know."

Pagan put her arm around the woman who had always fussed over her like a mother hen. "Maria, it's just a meal. Your cooking is always perfect. Is Ms. Van Zandt coming?"

"Yes, your uncle asked her last night. He seems to like her, doesn't he?"

Pagan laughed. "You mean romantically? I'm not sure my uncle even realizes she's a woman."

Maria wagged her finger. "Ah, Miss Pagan. Your uncle is still a man, I think. You wait and see."

Pagan climbed the stairs to her room. Maria had some funny ideas sometimes. Imagine her uncle in love. No, the idea was too preposterous. Not because of his age or anything like that, but because Mallory was married to his work. Anyone who knew him well knew that. Except Maria, of course.

She pulled open the closet door. Nothing there. She was really going to have to move out of her trailer this weekend. Actually, she guessed she'd already done that. Only, now she wanted her clothes to move out with her. She yanked a pullover sweater off the rack. Not much in the way of design, but it was clean. Now, for a quick shower, and she would be ready.

When she made her way downstairs forty-five minutes later, her uncle and their dinner guests had already arrived. She entered the drawing room unobtrusively from the side door. Her uncle, Theo, and the FBI agent were having a drink before dinner. She didn't have to listen in to their conversation to guess what they were discussing. So far no one had noticed her, giving her time to study the conferring agent sent to help solve the case.

Her first impressions were mixed. Swarthy, strong jawed, handsome, by most women's standards. Pagan knew better than to be taken in by lady-killers. She had learned long ago they were too smooth, too spoiled, and too full of themselves to be mistaken for real men. She watched him work his magic on her uncle and Theo—watched them hang on to his every word. This was going to be a long evening.

She walked farther into the room—far enough to attract attention. She had planned on completely ignoring him, but couldn't resist a sliding glance to see if he was watching. He was, and as she looked at him straight on, she suffered a jolt of unwanted recognition. This was the man with the Lexus. Those eyes—she wasn't very likely to forget them. She looked away, hoping he hadn't read her thoughts. It was unlikely he would remember her like she remembered him. She would just play it cool. Nothing would be said.

Her uncle looked up. "Pagan, come on in." He turned to the FBI man. "This is my niece, Pagan. Pagan, this is Demetri Ranoir." Pagan extended her hand to the stranger. He smiled, nodded, took her hand, then delivered the fatal blow. "You must be the criminal profiler your uncle was telling me about." His voice struck a chord in her memory that ricocheted erratically off the walls of her mind. Words stuck in her throat as their eyes locked. Her uncle began to explain the mistake, but they weren't listening. They were thinking back to the night before when he'd had his hand around her arm, and she had illegally entered a crime scene and examined vital evidence.

He let go of her hand, and she sat down. The rest of the evening was a blur. She guessed that she ate—she must have, mustn't she? But she was sure she didn't taste it. And talk? She must have talked, too. Was there such a thing as automatic talking? All she knew was that the one man who was all set to color her world was sitting across from her at the dining table—eating, talking, laughing, acting as if everything was normal—biding his time—searching for the perfect moment. She downed her glass of wine as if it were a shot and reached for another.

Sitting through that meal was like the long drive home when she was a kid. There she was—in trouble over some little shit rule that earned the words "when we get home, you're going to get a spanking." That's when the real punishment would begin—the miles and miles of fear and dread. She reached for another glass of wine, but the glass was empty—the bottle, missing.

He caught her eye and gave a slight nod. If he would have smiled or given her a smirk, she would have kicked him under the table no matter what the consequences. Her foot itched at the mere thought of it. Would this evening ever end? Right now, it seemed unlikely, yet years of experience told her it would.

Dessert was served in the living room with coffee. The wait was almost over. Distancing herself from the conversation, Pagan planned to wait out the rest of the evening in silence. Her uncle, however, had different plans, as she discovered when she heard her name brought into the conversation.

"Pagan has been helping me with a little background research on the victims. Doing quite a good job, I might add. She brought me a report yesterday on Tandy Gerald. Did you get a chance to find anything out on Nancy Starnes?"

Pagan took a sip of her coffee, uncomfortable at having all eyes centered on her—especially the pair colored Hershey chocolate brown. This was her chance to contribute—her chance to sound legitimate. "I interviewed her mother this morning. Did you know she was an artist? Nancy, I mean. The walls of her room are covered in her work."

Theo leaned slightly forward. "I get the feeling you found that significant. Have you discovered a link between the victims?"

"No, not yet, but I do think this might be important. Her painting is filled with the faces of people she knew. So, I asked Mrs. Starnes if Nancy had painted anything recently. She told me Nancy had added to the painting the weekend before she was killed."

"And you think the face of her killer might be in the mural?" Demetri guessed.

"Yes. I thought it was worth a shot. What do you think Uncle Mal?"

"I think it would be immensely helpful if it were. We might even find some of the other victims immortalized there. What were you planning to do?"

Pagan shifted in her chair, feeling suddenly self-conscious. She hadn't planned to reveal her plans publicly. "Well, I had hoped that we could get one of the photographers on staff to take some pictures of the walls and blow them up to be studied. Then, I could begin to identify the faces and see if anything showed up."

Mallory nodded, but it was Demetri who answered her. "I'd like to go with you tomorrow when the pictures are taken—see the wall for myself."

Pagan racked her brain for an excuse not to go. "I'm sure Ms. Starnes would be happy to show you the room. I'll be glad to give her a call."

Demetri ignored her comment and turned to her uncle. "You wouldn't mind if I borrowed her for tomorrow, would you? I'm sure Mrs. Starnes would feel much more comfortable with her along." He turned back to Pagan. "You wouldn't mind, would you?"

What could she say? "No, of course not."

"Good. I'll pick you up tomorrow morning at ten. You can fill me in on the way."

CHAPTER 8

▼

The two-story cedar house stood starkly gray against the deep blue sky of early evening. Build in the eighteen hundreds, the aging structure supported not only a turret with a steeple roof, but, also, a widow's walk leading out from a room-length balcony. Shingles hung loosely on the gabled roof in direct opposition to the shuttered windows, which were locked up tight. The balcony was never used now, and the widow's walk was boarded and chained, following the tragedy that had transpired thirty years earlier.

He walked through the house one last time before picking up the dainty white gloves from the hall table. "You'll see, Mama," he said, looking back over his shoulder. "I've gotten everything spotless this time—just like you like it."

"Did you wash the baseboards?"

"Yes, Mama. I cleaned the corners, too."

"You are a good boy."

"Yes, Mama. I take care of you, don't I?"

"Very good care, son."

He slipped the gloves over his hands. They were short and tight, but they would do. Then, with his hands outstretched, he walked around the room, checking the surfaces with his white gloves. If the gloves stayed clean, she would know how well he had done—how clean he had gotten the room.

A few minutes later, he took the gloves off, laying them in front of her. "See Mama. They're still clean." He watched her face break into a smile. "I picked you some roses, Mama." He brought the vase of flowers from the other room. "Your gardens are beautiful this year—bed after bed of red roses." The tears in her eyes melted his heart.

"You are the best son a mother could ask for."

Maria cleaned up the dinner table and brought Mallory his last cup of coffee. Guests gone, the atmosphere was back to the informality the old friends liked to maintain.

"Thank you, Maria. Aren't you having a cup?"

"I guess I could stop for a spell."

"Dinner was excellent. No one can touch your pot roast, you know."

"Well thanks, but do you think your guests enjoyed it?"

Mallory surprised her with a rare laugh. "Not like you to fish for a compliment. Cleaned their plates, didn't they? Yes, everyone loved it."

"Ms. Van Zandt seemed to enjoy herself. You've been seeing a good deal of her."

"Just to discuss the case. She's as much of a workaholic as I am."

Maria gave him a sly look, but let it drop. "And your FBI friend didn't let Pagan out of his line of sight very often."

"She wouldn't give him the time of day. Barely spoke to him."

"I noticed that, too. Odd, wasn't it? Almost like she had something against him."

"Maybe it was her way of punching him in the arm."

"You mean like in grade school? Hm…I wonder. There does seem to be something between them."

Sergeant Jamison knocked at the door of the red brick house for the third time, while Detective Gale Whiting looked around impatiently.

"I don't think anyone's home. Surely, they would have come to the door by now."

"Yeah, you're probably right. We'll try again later."

They were turning to walk off the porch, when the door suddenly opened.

"Can I help you?"

"Carl Hardwicke?"

"Yes, that's me."

"If you don't mind, we'd like to ask you a few questions. May we come in?"

"Sure. What's this all about?"

Gail followed Jimmy into the professor's living room. She was impressed. He had obviously used a decorator. Either that, or he had missed his calling. The place was exquisite from floor to ceiling. Beige blended with flashes of color to create a statement of taste and elegance without being gaudy.

After they were all seated, Jamison opened the conversation. "We are here about the murder of Carla Clumb. We understand you knew her."

"Yes, she was one of my students. I was so sorry to hear what happened."

"Would you have considered your relationship to have been close?"

"We had coffee a few times, but nothing serious. I don't make it a practice to date my students."

Gail looked up from her notes. "Actually, Mr. Hardwicke, we've been led to understand that is precisely your practice. That you have dated a number of your students."

The college teacher looked away. "Is my personal life part of your investigation?"

"Only if it concerns Ms. Clumb."

"I swear, we only had coffee."

Jamison decided to change tactics. "You are a published poet, are you not?"

"Yes, I am. Does that have something to do with the case?"

"Are there other published poets on the faculty?"

"Not that I know of. Is it important?"

"Probably not. Did Carla have a boyfriend?"

He shuffled uncomfortably. "I have no way of knowing that. How would I? Am I being accused of something?"

"No," Jamison said, standing up. "We appreciate your time. If there is anything else, we'll be in touch." He turned to leave without waiting for Whiting to follow.

They didn't speak until they were in the car. "Think he was telling the truth about Carla?"

Jamison gave her a look. "No, I don't. I think he's hiding something."

The grandfather clock chimed four a.m., but Theo's sleep was not disturbed. She was already awake. Her mind had been working overtime since the dinner party at Detective Mallory's house. Something was nagging at her. Something important. She just couldn't quite bring it to the surface.

Three women dead—young, beautiful women. Rose petals, poems, and pictures. Well, the pictures were an assumption, but he had to have some reason for applying the makeup and posing the bodies. Adorning the sacrifice? The practice wasn't unusual among ancient tribes.

The bodies were adorned, painted, and perfumed before burial, not for the people they left behind, but for the gods and goddesses the sacrifice was meant to appease. He was sacrificing these girls to someone—out of honor or maybe guilt. She was sure of it.

But there was something else. Something they really hadn't discussed—the cuts on the bodies. Maybe that was what was bothering her. The bodies had been cut post-mortem, but why? The autopsy hadn't been specific concerning any possible pattern. Was it a message? She must re-examine the autopsy photographs. Not many of them had been included in the files kept in the detective division.

Pagan faced the morning with a feeling of trepidation. Not only would she have to face Mrs. Starnes again, but would not be able to avoid a confrontation with Demetri Ranoir. She hated the doubt and uncertainty that came before a conflict, even though meeting the challenge in actual battle was often exhilarating. When he showed up in his Lexus, four cups of coffee later, she was ready.

Never one to be caught short, she decided the best defense was a good offense. Answering his knock at the door herself, instead of waiting for Maria, was her first move. He knocked—she appeared, and led the way to the car, getting inside before he had a chance to open the door for her. A raised eyebrow was his only reaction. She waited until he had fastened his seatbelt and started the motor before making her opening statements.

"You must feel really smug and pleased with yourself."

"Must I?" he answered, without turning his head.

His voice was cool—neutral, making her feel a little silly. "Are you going to turn me in?"

"For putting on lipstick at a stop sign?" he asked, pretending to misunderstand.

Was it possible he didn't recognize her from the other night? No. Absolutely not. "You know I am referring to the crime scene."

"The crime scene where the third body was found," he clarified. "I think I understand what happened. Your uncle is the detective in charge of the case, and as such, allows you to violate crime scenes and tamper with evidence."

His evaluation took her breath. She had never imagined her uncle might be blamed for her exploit. They had been traveling down Broadway and were now about two blocks from the station. He waited until he had pulled into the parking lot before continuing. "Is that about it? You know if I reported this, it would cost your uncle his job, not to mention what it would do to the integrity of the case."

Her mind raced with the implications of his words. She should never have brought the matter up, much less admitted her duplicity, admitted she was at the crime scene or handled the note. Now what? Was it too late to deny everything? It would be her word against his. Of course, he was a FBI agent, and she was what—an impulsive, silly, thoughtless…the adjectives just kept coming.

She looked up to see him watching her, studying her. What could she possibly say in her defense? In her uncle's defense? She had to convince him that her uncle was not involved. That the entire thing was her idea. He didn't look very open, but she had to try. Taking a deep breath, she tried to explain.

"Look. My uncle didn't know anything about it. I overheard the phone call, and wanted to see for myself. You see, I want to become an investigator, and I thought if I could discover something important about this case, he would take me seriously."

"Oh, I think he's going to view your actions very seriously. I know I do."

Her heart dropped into her stomach. He wasn't going to understand. He was going to be a hard-nose about it and try to destroy her and her uncle. What was she going to do? She just had to persuade him to let it drop.

"Okay. What I did was wrong, but I didn't hurt anything. No harm was done."

His eyes narrowed, and she noticed he was clenching his jaw. "You don't know that."

"I didn't do anything. That is what I keep telling you."

"You aren't listening to me." He unfastened his seatbelt and clutched the door handle. "Maybe you'll listen to the charges when they read them to you. Maybe sitting in a cell will give you some time to think about it."

"You're going to put me in jail?"

"Obstruction of justice is a serious charge, especially in an ongoing murder investigation."

She reached out to touch his arm. "Please don't do this. I understand. I won't ever do it again, I promise. Isn't there anything I can do to make up for it? Please. Just give me a chance."

He looked down at her hand lying against the sleeve of his coat. When he looked up his pupils were dilated almost to black. "What did you have in mind?" he asked in a low voice.

She wanted to jerk her hand away—pull it back and with it smack that look off his face. She didn't though. She had to buy some time and figure out what to do. Buying time was the name of the game. Forcing herself to smile, she moved her hand over until her fingers touched his leg. "I don't know. I thought maybe you could think of something."

He stared at her until she could feel the blood rushing into her face. "I'll think about it and let you know. Right now, we have a job to do."

Mallory arrived at the precinct early, needing some time to compose his thoughts before the briefing. The case was beginning to develop questions in all directions as bodies continued to appear. The facts were few and the questions, legion in number. They were learning more and more about the victims, but still knew almost nothing about the killer.

"Are you ready?" Theo asked, popping her head through the door.

"No, I'm not ready. In a few minutes I have to go in there and present a game plan, and I'm not sure I even know the game anymore. The more data we gather, the less we know."

Theo walked into the room. "I'm not sure that's accurate. Seems like more of an emotional evaluation than a factual one. Didn't you say Jamison and Whiting were interviewing a possible suspect?"

"One of our few leads. Meanwhile, the bodies keep piling up."

"Sooner or later he'll make a mistake. In the meantime, he'll keep you on track."

"What do you mean?"

"The murderer is playing out a very elaborate fantasy, and we have a part in that. We are his audience. We, alone, can witness his genius as well as his suffering. We got off course when we found the number three body before the number two, and he left us a note to help us out. Now we know he is watching us—keeping track of the investigation. If we take a wrong turn, he will send us a little help."

He stared at her a minute, while her words walked slowly through the corridors of his mind. "So, if he thought we weren't finding something he wanted us to find, then he would come out of his hiding place to give us some help."

"Yes. He is making a statement through his work, and he wants to be heard and understood."

"Sounds like you have a plan."

"Not a plan, but a couple of ideas."

A job to do? How was she supposed to keep fully focused on the job she needed to do with his threat hanging over her head? Her father had always maintained she would rather have a beating than have to wait. He was so right. And now what had she done? What had she promised to do? Nothing really. Nothing had been said, just implied. He couldn't expect to hold her to that, could he?

She sat unmoving as he exited the car and came around to open her door. Always the gentleman. Grabbing her bag, she followed him mechanically into the station. At least, she had bought herself some time, whatever the outcome. Her uncle was already in the briefing room, sitting at the front desk. She knew from what he had said the night before that this would be a meeting to review the case, present new information, and form a strategy. She felt out of place.

"I'll just wait out here."

Demetri gave her a quizzical look. "And miss the meeting? You wouldn't want to do that. Where is your sense of adventure? Is this the same woman who invaded a crime scene? Or does inviting you in make everything too simple. Maybe I should tell you not to come, and then you could sneak in later. Would that be more to your liking?"

She gave him a "go to hell" look, which seemed to further amuse him. Fine. He was determined to misconstrue her every thought and action. If she could just get through today, she wouldn't have to see him again. Who was she kidding? He had the means at his disposal to make her life hell for a long time to come.

CHAPTER 9

▼

Fanny pushed the screen door open wide, then stood aside, letting it close behind her with a bang. The morning was warm and bright, just right for exploring.

"Hurry up, Stevie. Did you bring your gun? There might be monsters."

"Bang. Bang. Where's my handcuffs?"

"You don't need them, come on."

"Yes, I do. We have to capture the bad guys."

Sheryl Sims watched them from the kitchen window. "Don't get out of the yard now," she yelled, knowing as soon as she said it that they would.

Fanny flipped around and gave her mother a half wave before turning once again to her brother. "Hurry, before Mama calls us again. We have to go."

"Where are we going anyway?"

"Right over there. Behind that building to look for treasure."

"There's treasure there?"

"Yeah, and maybe monsters. We better hide and sneak up."

"Okay, I got my gun ready."

"Follow me," Fanny ordered in a hushed voice, as she bent down low to avoid detection.

They hunkered down, keeping close to the building as they made their way across to the other side. Monsters surrounded them, and at one point, they were forced to fall back to avoid being eaten. That was when Stevie raised his gun and began to shoot. "Bang, bang, bang," he shouted, twisting this way and that. The enemy fell before him, dropping dead in their tracks. It was in this manner that Fanny and Stevie made their way to the front of the building and saw the stranger. Fanny froze flat against the building, while Stevie held his gun out threateningly.

"You're not going to shoot me with that, are you son?"

"Bang, bang, bang."

This exchange propelled Fanny into action. She stepped between Stevie and the stranger to protect her brother. "We're not supposed to talk to strangers," she said, placing her hands on her hips to demonstrate the strength of her position.

The man smiled. "Oh, I'm not a stranger. I live right down the street. I'm one of your neighbors."

"What are you doing here?" she persisted, unconvinced.

He hesitated before answering. "Well, I am an artist, and I was finishing a piece of my work."

"Where is it?" Stevie piped up, curiosity overcoming his fear of talking to a stranger.

"In there." He pointed through the window inside the house.

Both children ran over to look, noses pressed against the glass.

"Looks like a big Barbie doll. What is that all over her?"

"Rose petals."

"Pretty. Can we go in and look?"

"Sure. I have a couple of more things to do. You can help me if you want."

"Oh boy. We get to help. This is going to be fun."

The meeting had lasted over two hours, and by the time it was over, Pagan felt drained and overwhelmed by the volume of information she had received. What she knew before seemed insignificant compared to what she had learned. What a fool she had been to think she could make a difference. How did she think she could find him when all the people in that room working together couldn't?

She looked over to where Demetri was talking to the photography crew, explaining what he wanted from the shot. He looked decisive—in charge. He doesn't really need me. This case doesn't need me. He was right. I don't know what I'm doing, and I'm in the way. By the time he joined her, she had decided to go home.

They didn't speak on the way back to his car, neither of them willing to break the uneasy wall of silence between them. When they reached the passenger side of the car, he held the door and she slid into the seat without acknowledging his gesture of Southern courtesy. They belted up, and he reached for the key. They rode for the first several miles in silence. Finally, finding the tension unbearable, she cleared her throat and said what was uppermost in her mind.

"I want to go home. I'm not going back to the Starnes's house."

He sat back in the seat. "May I ask why?"

"You know why. You said it yourself. I don't know what I'm doing, and I'm in the way."

"That's not what I said, but I can see how this would fit right into your usual pattern."

"What's that supposed to mean?"

"You start something, and at the first bump in the road, you quit and start something else. Nine jobs in three years, didn't your uncle say last night at dinner? Well, it's not going to be that simple this time. This is one project you're going to see through to the end."

The unsaid "or else" hung in the air between them, making any further discussion on the subject redundant. Fine. She would go but she wouldn't do anything. She would just stand around and look bored. And probably be bored. What a tough break. Finally, found a job she enjoyed, and he had to ruin it. On the other hand, why should she let him destroy it for her? He was the outsider not her. There was only one thing for her to do.

Funny how eliminating options can change your perspective. He wanted her to see this through. She would see this through, all right. He thought she had done this on a whim—that she was an immature kid who didn't know her own mind. Well, she would show him what she could do. After all, wasn't she the one who discovered the note about the missing girl? And wasn't she the one who discovered the painting on the wall?

By the time they reached the Starnes's house her mind was made up. She practically leapt out of the car when he shifted it into park and led the way to the front door, leaving him to follow in her dust. She knocked on the door, wanting to talk to Mrs. Starnes before the photographers had finished unpacking their equipment. The door opened almost immediately.

"Mrs. Starnes. I hate to bother you again, but we are very interested in Nancy's painting. We would like to take photographs of it to study, if that's all right with you?"

"Well, I don't know. It is kind of private—personal."

Pagan spoke up before Mrs. Starnes could resist even further. "Mrs. Starnes, I understand your feelings, but this may be the clue we need to solve Nancy's case. We are interested in the faces she drew on the wall."

Mrs. Starnes pressed her hands against her mouth. "Oh, my god. You think the face of the killer could be there, don't you?"

"We have to consider all possibilities. May we go up?"

58   Red Red Rose

Mrs. Starnes motioned toward the stairs and left the room.

Mallory hung up the phone without saying a word, but Theo knew. They had been working for about an hour when the ringing started. The first call was from the watch commander. He had received some information he thought Mallory should be made aware of. Mallory had listened, told him to keep him up to date, but had not explained the call. Ten minutes later the phone rang again. "Bring it to me," was all he said. Theo watched him attempt to hide his emotions under a poker face. Apparently poker was not his game.

"When are you going to tell me, Mal? I'm not fragile, you know."

He looked up, meeting her eyes over the papers in his hand. "Sometimes I think I am the fragile one. Each death seems harder and harder to accept."

"They have discovered another body?"

"Not yet, but we have strong reason to believe one exists."

Her next remark was interrupted when the door opened and Jamison handed a folder to Mallory. After a brief glance, he handed the inside paper to Theo.

"What is this?" she asked, clearly puzzled by what she saw.

Mallory motioned to Jamison, who was now standing beside the desk.

"We got this fax about an hour ago. We have traced the initiating machine to a library computer. The fax itself gives us little clue as to where the picture was taken or when."

"Do we have an ID on the children?"

"No. We don't know who they are, where they live, or even if they are still alive."

Theo tried not to look as alarmed as she felt. "We can't assume the worst. His bent doesn't include children."

"Or hasn't so far," Mallory observed.

Demetri walked into the bedroom, not really knowing what to expect. Pagan waited by the door, not wanting to in any way, disrupt his first impressions of the artwork. He examined each of the walls without comment before motioning the camera crews in to set up.

"Your instincts were right, Pagan," he said, surprising her with the use of her name.

"In what way?"

"The painting should be examined—even if the face isn't there. This may be the break we were looking for."

"But it may be a waste of time."

"Maybe, but that's what detectives do. The good ones, anyway. Did you examine the rest of the room?"

Her eyes darted around the room. Drat. Just when she seemed to be making some points. "No. After I saw the painting, I...uh, No. I didn't examine the rest of the room."

"Start at the dresser, and I'll take the chest of drawers. Wear the gloves."

She breathed out a long sigh. When did this volunteer work become a job with a boss? Took some of the fun out, not to mention the spontaneity.

The dresser was just what she would have expected of a college student. Photos stuck between the mirror and the frame outlined her reflection. She wondered if she should bring them to the station to be checked out. Reaching for a plastic evidence bag, she removed the pictures along with a packet of letters bound with a ribbon. Nothing else seemed significant until she opened the bottom drawer. A diary. At first, she didn't even want to touch it. Seemed like such a personal thing, but if it would help them find the killer.... She picked up the diary and added it to the bag. Then, she handed it to Demetri, who had joined her beside the mirror.

"This looks interesting. The chest was full of clothes, nothing else. Let's check the closet and then go back to the station."

"What do you want us to do?"

Mallory answered Jamison's question with another question. "Any word from the team at Starnes's house?"

"They're on their way back."

"Good. Jamison, would you ask Whiting to join us, and make me ten extra copies of this fax." As Jamison left the room, Mallory turned to Theo. "We've got some tough decisions to make and not a lot of time to make them."

Jamison and Whiting came back into the room cutting off any private remark he might have added. Mallory waited until they were seated before continuing, picking up the copies Jamison put on the desk.

"First, is there anything we might have missed in the faxed picture? Anything in the background?"

Whiting spoke first. "What are they in? Is it a garage?"

"I can't tell from this. It just isn't clear enough."

Mallory sat the picture back on the desk. "All right. What next? Television spots? Is that our only alternative? Theo?"

She stood up beside the desk. "Mallory and I had been talking about flushing this guy out by letting him think we missed some of his clues. Then, he would be forced to communicate with us more directly—like the note Pagan found at the last scene."

Pagan and Demetri entered the room just in time to catch the tail end of Theo's remark. Pagan looked up to find Demetri staring at her, his look judgmental, condemning. Theo paused as they made their way to the back of the room before continuing.

"Well, that won't be feasible now. We must use every means at our disposal to locate those kids as quickly as possible—television, newspapers, word of mouth. We don't know if he's just pulling our string here or if the kids are in real danger, but they've got to be our first priority, even if it means losing a chance to trap the killer."

"I think television. That has to be the fastest way of getting the picture out. Is everyone agreed?" Mallory waited until everyone had nodded. "Most of you have met Agent Ranoir. Demetri, do you have anything else to add?"

Demetri stood up as Theo took her seat. "I think the information you give out at this point is going to be crucial. My advice is to say as little as possible about the case. In fact, I don't think the case should be mentioned, just that we're seeking the identity of the kids."

"People are going to want some sort of explanation."

"I have an idea on that," Theo interjected. "Let's just say they have some information we need, pertinent to the solving of a case, making the plea very strong."

Mallory waited only a moment before giving the order. Jamison, acting as his trusty second, was in charge of seeing it was carried out. Mallory, meanwhile, called a meeting to brief the rest of the squad.

"Theo, I'd like you to be there fielding questions. Demetri, how'd it go at the Starnes's house? Did you find anything significant to the case?"

"We have some evidence that looks promising. I had hoped to take a closer look following our meeting here."

"Sure. You and Pagan go ahead. There's no reason for you to attend the briefing. You're both up to speed on what's going on. I'd like to see anything you come up with as soon as possible."

"Sure, we'll get right on it," he said, turning to Pagan. "Take a half hour or so for lunch, then meet me in my office."

"You have an office?"

"A consulting office right down the hall. I'll be expecting you."

The break room, which also served as a workroom, was located on the second floor of the building. The snack machines against the back wall of the room contained sandwiches as well as chips and sweets. What more could a girl ask for? After making her selections, which included a Diet Coke from the bright red drink machine, Pagan's lunch was complete.

Moving to one of the white plastic tables close to the vending station, she sat down and unwrapped her lunch. Most of the other men and women in the room wore uniforms and firearms. The effect was disconcerting and more than a little intimidating. She felt like a lamb among wolves as she sipped on her Diet Coke under their watchful eyes. Not that they were openly staring, but the curious, suspicious glances she was getting did little to improve her appetite.

She was in the process of clearing her table when the first pictures of the unidentified children flashed across the television screen. The faxed picture had been enhanced and colorized, but the fuzzy image would still be hard for someone to positively identify. By the time she reached the ground floor and Agent Ranoir's office, the first calls were already coming in.

CHAPTER 10

▼

Pagan's knock sounded timid against the heavy oak door, but the order to come in was immediate. She found Ranoir seated at his desk surrounded by the bag of evidence taken from Nancy Starnes's bedroom. From the little blue stickers on each item, she knew they had already been tagged and examined for fingerprints. Demetri gave her a brief glance before turning back to the work before him. Pagan took the seat directly in front of the desk and waited.

"You've finished lunch?" he asked, without looking up.

"Yes."

"Good. I want you to read through these letters. On the table to your right are the yearbooks from the school Nancy attended. After you finish the letters, I want you to take these pictures, match them to their names, and make me a list. Think you can do that?"

She took the letters from his outstretched hand. "Is that a rhetorical question?"

He smiled for the first time since the dinner at her uncle's house. The change was quite an improvement, making him look almost amiable. "Yes," he said answering her question.

For the next twenty minutes she read the letters. Silly, girlie writing with hearts and flowers scrawled across the pages. When she had finished, she turned to the yearbooks. What she really wanted was the job he had kept for himself, the reading of Nancy's diary.

Mallory was almost finished with the briefing when the calls hit the switchboard. The officers manning the phones took down the information quickly and efficiently, passing it on if it seemed important, cataloging it if it didn't. Soon, the entire force was busy checking leads and processing information. Mallory had just re-entered his office when the call came through giving an address for the children.

In only a matter of minutes the case team along with a forensic team was on route to the house. While the forensic team waited in the van, Mallory and Theo went to the door, leaving the other case team members stationed within calling distance. The children's mother met them at the door, noticeably upset, her shrill voice articulating her concerns loudly enough for both teams to hear.

"What's this all about? My kids ain't done nothing wrong. Why's their picture plastered all over the TV like they was criminals or something?"

Mallory took over the introductions himself. "Ma'am, are these your children?" At her nod he continued. "My name is Augustus Mallory with the Tyler Police Department. We were sent pictures of your children with some information, leading us to believe they might be in danger. Are the children here with you now?"

The woman looked behind Mallory at the large collection of police personnel. "What are they doing here?"

"Just a precaution, Ma'am, in case the children needed our help."

She looked back over her shoulder and yelled, "Fanny. Stevie. Come down here for a minute."

As Mallory and the team waited, two tow-headed children appeared around the skirt of the woman in the doorway. He recognized them immediately as the children from the photograph. Calling Jamison on his hand-held, he gave the order to call off the television ads and begin an area search. Then, he re-addressed the woman.

"I'm sorry, what is your name?"

"Sims. Mrs. Harry Sims."

"Mrs. Sims. May we come in and talk to you and your children? I would like to explain what this is all about and apologize for any inconvenience we may have caused you."

After a brief hesitation, the woman agreed and moved away from the doorway. Mallory and Theo followed.

The white frame house was small, but neat. Mrs. Sims led them to the kitchen table and sat down, moving the morning paper to clear a space.

"Now, what is this all about?"

Theo pulled a copy of the fax out of her briefcase. He nodded.

The woman stared at the picture. "Where did this come from? How did you get this?"

"Mrs. Sims, a couple of hours ago we received this photo at the police station on our fax. We need to know where your children were when this picture was taken."

"Fanny, Stevie, come here." The children left the doorway where they had been watching the team conduct a physical search of the area. "When was this picture taken, Fanny?"

"Wow, that's me and Stevie. Look, Stevie. There we are. And there's the Barbie doll."

"What Barbie doll?" Mrs. Sims snatched the paper away from her daughter. Holding the paper closer to her face, she re-examined the photo. "Oh, my god," she said, putting her hand over her mouth as the horror of revelation distorted her features. Then, dropping the paper on the table, she clutched her children to her, until they cried out in protest.

"Mrs. Sims." Theo left her chair to kneel in front of the frightened woman. "Now you understand why we were so concerned and why we must find out everything we can about what happened to the children."

She nodded. "Fanny, where is the Barbie doll?"

Fanny gave her a sly look. "It's a secret, Mommy. The nice man said not to tell."

Mrs. Sims put her arm around her daughter's shoulders. "Fanny, we don't have secrets from the police. We can tell them anything."

Fanny looked around. "Where are they? Where are the policemen?"

Her mother made a sweeping gesture. "These nice people are policemen."

Fanny shook her head. "No, policemen wear police uniforms. These people just have regular clothes."

Mallory pulled out his cell phone and dialed. "Jenkins—Mallory. Get me a couple of uniforms to the Sims's house right away. Use the sirens."

Fanny clapped her hands. "We're going to get to see some real policemen?"

"That's right," Mallory assured her. "Would you like to see my badge?"

"Sure. Will I still get to see the policemen?"

"Yes, they're on their way."

As Theo watched the little girl grow more and more trusting, she wondered about the long-term effects of murder. What about five years from now? Ten— when the little girl understood about the Barbie doll and who her new friend really was? How would the information affect her then?

Fanny and Stevie's excitement at seeing the uniformed policemen was heart-warming. To be so innocent. Mallory addressed the uniformed men. "Fanny has a secret to share with you. Go ahead, Fanny. Policemen protect secrets."

Fanny smiled. "I guess I can trust you, but I'll have to whisper. I'm going to tell you where the Barbie doll is."

The policeman played along. "Maybe you could show me, Fanny."

"All right. Come on, Stevie. Let's show the policeman the Barbie doll."

Five minutes later Mallory viewed the body of the fourth victim. Like the others, it was covered in red rose petals. Also like the others, the girl was heavily made up. He looked around for the neat pile of clothes he knew would be sitting beside the body. They had been placed in the far corner—pants on top with the underwear inside covering the note. He donned his plastic gloves and removed the note, which like all the previous notes contained a cryptic poem. Mallory scanned it hurriedly.

A gentle touch upon my brow
A kindly word was said
My lovely girl's not with me now,
My lovely girl is dead.

Her sun-kissed cheeks are pale and wan
Her smooth, warm skin grown cold
She still looks now as she did then,
She never will grow old.

"Why?" you say. "What is my cause?
What is my course to run?"
What demons haunt me you will know
My hell and yours are one.

* * * *

The house was cold—wind whistling through withered wood shrunk long ago by the mutual efforts of neglect and elemental forces. He walked across the wooden floor in his bare feet—grown numb from chilled air seeping through widened cracks—seeking rugs threadbare from too much washing. Woven floor

66   Red Red Rose

throws she had made in the day. Memories of happiness captured in cloth—time capsules of their world together. His sigh puffed white in the chill morning air, and he hugged his arms against his body in attempted rebuttal. The fire was dead—flaky gray ash settled into shapeless heaps where heat had long ago escaped.

Building a fire became his one priority, his passion. Lovely, lovely fire. Warmth, heat, beauty—she often came to him in the firelight. When the house was dark and still, the flickering flames would form tendrils of golden long hair framing her face—and they would talk. About them, about life, about what wouldn't be and could have been. About death.

Death took her. Stole her before her time. Used its sharp knife to cut out his heart. Death had become his enemy, his nemesis—but not his conqueror. He had discovered a way to beat death at its own game. Rob it of its power—vanquish it forever. He became one with his worst enemy—became death itself. Then, and only then could he win.

As fire started to catch, curls of smoke rose from the ashes, life from death, the Phoenix rising from the flames. He huddled close, remembering.

The day was cold—cold and wet. He had wanted to sleep in, but she said they had to get up—prepare for the snow and ice that would surely come. He had clung to her that day and she to him as if somehow they knew it would be the last.

Fresh baked biscuits filled the morning air with the smell of yeast. They laughed as they ate—sharing and loving—tiny moments of life to cherish. Her smile was infectious—a sweet disease from which he'd never recovered. He smiled back, content to be with her—to love and be loved by her. They ate the buttered bread with homemade jam. She missed a spot of red at the corner of her mouth, and he laughed. She used the tip of her finger to move it to the end of her nose and made a face. He laughed even more then. She liked that—to hear him laugh. She threw her arms around him and hugged.

"You're my boy," she said, "my best boy."

Pagan studied the photos of the painted wall. While the case team was examining facts surrounding the latest victim and trying to make an identification, she was supposed to match the faces with any yearbook photos she could find. The work was tedious, but rewarding, and it kept her mind from obsessing over her own situation.

So far, working with FBI agent Ranoir had been uneventful—at least as far as her situation was concerned. Nothing else had been said about her infractions.

He had been courteous, but distant—speaking only when necessary, avoiding her if possible. Not that she was complaining. She didn't want to spend time with him any more than he did with her. The sanctimonious prick. So, she had taken a few short cuts and broken a few rules. Hadn't the good she'd done made up for that? Evidently not—not in his opinion anyway.

Fine. She would accept whatever punishment she was due, but not her uncle. That wasn't fair. Her uncle was not responsible for her behavior. Ranoir knew that. It was a bluff—a way to get to her—to scare her. At least she hoped it was.

She opened the yearbook of Nancy's senior year and turned to the back section. Row after row of kids whose future looked bright. Teenagers poised at the pinnacle of hope, dreaming of sugarplums and yellow-bricked roads. How could they know? How could they even imagine it might be over before it had time to begin?

As she looked at the pictures, recognition dawned, and she began to list the names. The girls were the easiest. Maybe because she didn't have to view them as suspects. At the end of the first hour, she had listed eleven names, including Mrs. Starnes who looked out at her from behind the leaves of the giant Magnolia tree.

Theo Van Zandt studied the photographs taken at the site, then looked back at the fax. "He is enjoying this, you know?"

"The killing?" Mallory questioned.

"The collaboration. We have added a new element to his mission—the discovery—the analysis. He doesn't feel so alone anymore. He has us—his audience. We are his fans, his critics, his admirers."

Jamison spoke up, his shaking head confirming his denial. "No, we are his hunters."

"Yes," Gail agreed. "We are his hunters, but I think what Theo is saying is that he doesn't view us that way. He doesn't feel hunted. And I guess that means he doesn't feel fear either." She looked to Theo for confirmation.

"Yes, that's right. Fear is not his motivating factor, and neither is survival. If it were, he would have killed the children."

"Maybe killing children violates his sense of morality," Jamison speculated.

"Killing Janet Stevimeyer didn't seem to bother him," Gail said, turning toward him.

"Maybe he doesn't see the children as a threat. Doesn't think them capable of identifying him."

"That's possible of course. But would he even take that chance if he were worried about possible apprehension? I don't think he cares."

Mallory stepped forward. "Then, why is he so careful at the crime scenes? Why doesn't he leave us more clues?"

Theo smiled. "I didn't say he wanted to get caught. I said he didn't fear it. There is a big difference."

Demetri Ranoir brought the autopsy report into the room. "No surprises here. The kids must have turned up at the scene right after it happened. When are they scheduled to come in for the ID?"

Mallory looked at his watch. "They should be here now."

"You mean to have Carl Hardwicke in the line-up?"

"Yes, as our number one suspect. We hope the kids can provide the positive ID we need."

"But you don't expect it, do you?" Ranoir continued.

"No, I don't. His alibis are too well substantiated."

CHAPTER 11

▼

Jamison watched Carl Hardwicke through the two-way mirror. Hardwicke had been sitting in the investigation room for about five minutes and was becoming restless. Let him stew for a while. Maybe he'll be more liable to make mistakes later. He waited about five more minutes before entering the room.

"Hello, Sergeant. Decided you had watched me squirm long enough? You are violating my civil rights, you know. I had alibis for the times of the murders. You had no cause to bring me in for questioning, and you know it."

"Just relax, Hardwicke. This is routine. We are bringing in a lot of people acquainted with the victims for questioning."

Hardwicke settled back in his seat. "So, what do you want to know?"

Jamison gave the man seated across from him a long look. Mousy brown hair fell in lanky strings covering a hairline that had long since receded. The lines in his face were weak—too many easy breaks—too little ambition. "I want to know more about your relationship with Carla."

"Look, like I told you before, we only had coffee a few times. If that's all you want me for, then am I free to go?"

"Not quite yet. Are you familiar with the Rose Tree Motel, Mr. Hardwicke?"

"I know it's located on Fifth Street by the Taco Bell."

"You know a good deal more than that, sir. For instance, you know that on April sixteenth, you checked in with a young woman who the clerk has identified as Carla Clumb. He said he had seen you and the young woman several times before. Care to comment on that?"

"You have no real proof that it was Carla."

- 69 -

70   Red Red Rose

"Don't I? Would you rather answer these questions in front of a jury? Wonder what effect that would have on your career?"

"Go to hell."

"Is that your final answer? Okay, I'll see you in court."

"Okay, okay. So, Carla and I hung out a few times. What of it?"

"By *hung out* you mean you had intercourse?"

"Yes, we had sex. All right? Are you happy now? Doesn't mean I killed her."

"No, but it means you lied. How long did you and Carla *hang out?*"

"Not long. 'Bout three months, I guess. Wasn't serious. We just had a few laughs. She was a good person. Didn't deserve what happened to her. I hope you catch the son of a bitch."

"We intend to. There is something you can do for us, though."

"Yeah, what's that?"

"We need to officially rule you out. I'd like you to stand in a line up."

Hardwicke shook his head. "And if I refuse?"

"I can force you—making you look guilty as hell. Don't refuse."

"Fine. When?"

"Now. Give me a few minutes, and I'll come to get you."

Pagan picked up the diary from Ranoir's desk. She had gone as far as she could with the pictures and needed a break. Besides, she had wanted to read the diary ever since she had discovered it. Ranoir had flipped through it a couple of times, but had never acted interested. Surely, he wouldn't mind if she took a peek. After all, she was working on the case. Thinking to cut to the chase, she opened to the back of the book and began to read.

"Tuesday, June 4th—This new job is such a bore. Answering the phone all day in a cheery vacuous voice makes me feel automated, like the proverbial cog in the wheel. Guess that's what I am. I've even been answering my home phone like that lately. How embarrassing. My friends all think it's a hoot."

"Friday, June 7th—Billy called. We talked over an hour, but he didn't ask me out. Guess I blew it when I told him I only wanted to be friends. Fine time for him to believe me. I am allowed to change my mind, aren't I? He was cute. I thought so then, but I was dating someone else. Not now. Now, would be an excellent time for him to call."

"Wednesday, June 8th—My first bouquet of flowers arrived earlier this evening. Roses. I love red roses. Sweet, sweet boy. He has always been so thoughtful. Why wasn't he the one I feel in love with?"

Pagan closed the book. Starting at the end wouldn't be of any help. She would have to read through from the beginning. Were the roses from the killer? And if so, was his picture painted on the wall?

Mallory watched as Fanny and Stevie entered the station holding firmly to their mother's hands—their eyes big and round as they stared openly at the many uniforms and badges surrounding them. Shrinking closer to their mother was as natural as the way their tiny hands gripped hers.

"Mama, are we going to get arrested?"

"Are they going to put us in jail?"

Their mother squatted down beside them. "No, Fanny we're not going to be arrested, and we're not going to be put in jail, Stevie. We're just going to visit with the nice policemen. In fact, we are going to help them."

"How?"

"Well, by telling them about yesterday and what you saw."

"Oh boy, we'll be like real policemen. Will we get a gun?"

"No," she answered Stevie, standing back up. "But you will be a lot of help anyway."

Mallory approached the trio. "Welcome Mrs. Sims, Fanny, Stevie. If you'll follow me I'll take you on a quick tour of the department."

Fanny and Stevie bombarded him with questions for the next fifteen minutes as they were introduced to officers around the station. By the time they had finished their rounds, the kids were completely over their fear of uniforms and badges. The last room they visited was the interrogation room. Mallory waited until everyone was seated before beginning the questioning.

"Fanny, can you tell us what you did after you left your house yesterday morning?"

Fanny sat up, looking smug and important. She looked around to reassure herself that all eyes were on her before beginning her story. Jamison and Whiting watched her through the two-way mirror, aware that she and the boy were the only living witnesses to have ever seen the killer.

Jamison leaned toward Whiting, whispering, as if the people on the other side of the glass could hear. "Think she'll be able to come up with anything useful?"

"No, not really. But who knows? Children sometimes catch things adults miss."

"These kids might just wrap up the entire case for us."

"Wouldn't that be nice?"

72 Red Red Rose

Their conversation was interrupted as Fanny began to speak. "Well, me and Stevie left the house to play spy. Mama said not to leave the yard so we just went across the alley to the white house behind us. We sneaked around to the front and saw the man."

"What did he look like?"

"He was big," supplied Stevie, determined not to be left out.

"Yeah, he was real big—like a monster."

"No, he wasn't. He wasn't like a monster. He looked like a policeman."

Mallory turned to Stevie. "Was he wearing a uniform?"

"No."

"Then, why did he look like a policeman?"

"I don't know. He just did."

"Did he look like any of the policemen you met today?"

Stevie looked around. "Yes, all of them. He was big."

Mrs. Sims looked embarrassed. "I'm sorry. He watches too much TV."

Mallory turned back to Fanny. "Fanny, did you notice anything about the man?"

"He had a camera and he took our pictures. He was very nice. He showed us the big doll. She had a red dress made of flowers. I wish I had a dress like that."

Mallory forced a smile. "Do you remember what he looked like?"

"Yes, I remember."

"Did he have any hair?" Mallory prompted.

Fanny shrugged. "I guess. He had on a hat."

"A hat like a police hat?"

"No, no," Stevie yelled, getting frustrated. "A hat like a baseball player wears, silly."

"Stevie," Mrs. Sims corrected. "It's not nice to call people silly."

Mallory ignored the interruption. "Do you think you would recognize the man again, if you saw him?"

"Sure, we would. Wouldn't we, Stevie?"

At Stevie's enthusiastic nod, Mallory gave the signal for the setup. A few minutes later the kids were lead to the room where they would view the line of men, including Carl Hardwicke. The children watched closely as the men were led across the stage, excited by the novelty of the entire experience. They didn't move as the men were ordered to turn to the left and then to the right.

"Do any of these men look like the man with the Barbie doll?"

"Are they on TV?"

C. Rowe-Myers 73

"No. One of the men may have been the man who took your picture," Mallory explained.

"Which one?" Fanny asked.

Mallory took a deep breath. "I was hoping you could tell me. Do any of these men look like the man who took your picture?"

"No," Fanny answered.

"I think they all do," Stevie added.

Mallory leaned down to the microphone. "That will be all Sergeant. The men can be dismissed."

Jamison took his time making his way to Hardwicke's cell. So the kids didn't identify him. Didn't mean he didn't do it. Hardwicke stood up as he came near, the man's sneer firmly in place.

"You needn't look so smug, Hardwicke. You're not off the hook, yet."

"You've got nothing on me. I'll sue you for everything you're worth. This is harassment. You'll be hearing from my lawyer."

Jamison opened the cell door. "Yada, yada, yada. We'll be watching your every move. Sooner or later you'll screw up, and we'll be there. Let's go."

Pagan stepped out of the room where she had just spent the last three hours. She stretched and looked down the hall, hoping to locate something familiar. Heading right, she moved quickly down the tiled hallway and opened the door leading into the main room of the station. The room's main activity was centered at the raised dais in the middle of the room. Looking neither to the left or the right, she walked straight toward the glass-bordered partition, barely avoiding a headlong crash into Carl Hardwicke. He never slowed down or gave any indication he noticed her or was aware of their near miss. Muttering a string of expletives, he continued with a rapid stride and exited the room. Pagan, however, didn't move for a long minute, not until a hand at her elbow broke the spell evoked by the rude stranger.

"Are you all right?"

"Who was that man?" she asked, giving Demetri a brief glance.

"Carl Hardwicke, our prime suspect in the *Rose* murders."

"We're not holding him?"

"No evidence. He passed the line-up, and he has firm alibis for the times of the murders. Why?"

Pagan gave herself a mental shake. "I don't know. Maybe I'm just confused, but I'm almost positive his face is one of the ones I saw on Nancy Starnes's painted wall."

Jamison slammed the file folder down on the table. "How many women have to die before we can get this pervert?"

"Maybe it's not him. How do we know for sure? All we really know is that he writes poetry and that he dated Carla Clumb. Might have been unethical, but it hardly makes him a murderer." Whiting flipped open the folder to the first case, Tandy Gerald. "These girls have to have something in common. What? What are we missing? And what do you make of the letter he cuts into them—the 'A?' Do you think it stands for adultery as in *The Scarlet Letter* or is that a bit obvious?"

"Maybe we should start with a list of things it could stand for. I'll write down the word 'adultery' at the top. You do a list of your own, and we'll compare over supper."

"Are you asking me out, Jamison?"

"Are you accepting, Whiting?"

She paused only briefly. "Sure. Why not? I could use a break. Pick me up at seven?"

"I'll be there. Be sure and bring your list."

Demetri followed Pagan into the office, waiting until she had retrieved the photographs before speaking. "You know how important this would be if you are right. We would have a definite tie between at least two of the murders."

She flipped through the eight by ten glossies twice before stopping. The section she held was the one depicting the upper branches of some of the smaller trees. The limbs were thin—lapping over each other in their bid for a clear shot at the sun. Faces peered through the leaves—uncertain and indistinct—fading and emerging alternately with every look. She was beginning to think she had imagined the entire image when suddenly she saw it plainly peering out of the shadows.

"Here, look right here."

He stepped behind her, looking over her shoulder. After a minute, he saw it too. She was right. The painting did resemble Hardwicke. Ranoir walked over to stand behind his desk. Well, it was what he had been waiting for, wasn't it? His big break—the clue he needed to put his plan into action. Only now, using Pagan as bait to catch the killer didn't sound like such a great idea. Too many unknowns. What if something went wrong—something that would culminate in a photograph of Pagan lying forever still, covered in red rose petals?

Pagan looked up. "Something wrong? It's Hardwicke, isn't it?"

"Looks like it." He sat down, folding his hands atop the desk. "We need to talk."

She laid the picture on the table, sensing the photo was not to be the main topic of conversation. "What do you want to talk about?"

"I believe you owe me for my continued silence concerning a certain indiscretion you committed while working on this case. I have found a way for you to make amends."

His words hit her like a jolt of lightening. The sudden panic she felt spread through her system like a fast acting poison, painful—leaving numbness in its wake. Her face revealed none of what she was feeling, remaining deceptively blank. "And can I assume that my making amends will wipe the slate clean not for only myself, but for my uncle as well?"

"Yes, of course."

"What assurances would I have?"

"I would give you my word."

"And that is supposed to convince me?"

He gave her a look she could only interpret as arrogant. "It will have to do."

She splayed her fingers across the table in front of her, buying time before she asked the all-important question. "So, what do you want me to do?"

"You're going to ferret out our killer."

"And how do you propose I do that? As an FBI spy?"

He looked at her directly before answering, locking blue eyes with brown. "As bait."

CHAPTER 12

▼

Jamison looked at the directions to Whiting's apartment. Upscale area for a cop's salary. Wonder if she's on the take. There's no law saying only men can be dirty. He rounded the final corner to bring him in front of her door. Number 35A. A glassed-in flower box differentiated her apartment from those surrounding it. A homey touch, sadly out of place with her structured, uniformed life.

His knock at the door was hesitant. Gail Whiting was the closest thing to a partner he had—the closest thing to a friend. He wouldn't want to ruin their relationship with unforeseen complications. Maybe this was a really bad idea. The door opened just as he was turning to go.

"Changing your mind?" Gail asked, her voice holding more than a hint of amusement.

He looked at her closely before answering. The slinky red dress transformed her from a sometimes-gawky female police officer into a desirable woman. "God, Gail. Who knew?"

"You like?"

"What red-bloodied American male wouldn't? You clean up real nice, Lady."

"Right back at ya."

Jamison laughed and offered his arm. "If I'd known you were hiding this under that uniform, I'd asked you out earlier."

"I resent that, Jimmy. I'd prefer to think you asked me out for your interest in my mind."

He gave her a crooked grin. "Yeah, that was it. That's exactly what I meant. Hungry?"

"Starved."

"Anything special in mind?"

"Hm....A steak would be nice."

"My thought exactly," he agreed assisting her into the car. "You smell sweet, like roses."

Gail turned her head. "Now, you're reaching. Everyone knows roses don't smell."

"Au contraire. Tea roses don't often smell, but that is only one variety. Many types of roses have a wonderful smell and have for centuries."

"A rose fan, huh? And I always had you figured as the macho type."

"Be hard to grow up in the Rose City and not know something about roses, now wouldn't it? We didn't start out with roses, you know. During the early twentieth century, cotton was the leading cash crop, then later in the century truck farming and fruit orchards took over the spotlight. By the 1900's there were over one million fruit trees in the area."

"Really? I never knew that. What kind of fruit?"

"Mainly peach. But when a peach blight wiped out much of the fruit industry, many farmers turned to growing roses. This time they struck gold. The flower proved ideally suited to the climate and soil of the Tyler area."

"So, that's why we're called the Rose Capital of the World?"

"No, not exactly. By the 1920s the rose industry had developed into a major business, and by the 1940s more than half the U.S. supply of rose bushes was grown within ten miles of Tyler. That's why."

"Wow, I'm really impressed you know so much. How do you know so much?"

He laughed. "My grandmother used to work in the nurseries during the summer. She talked about it a lot. Kind of grew up with it."

Jamison pulled off the highway into the parking lot of the Red Barn Steak House. Gail waited patiently while he circled the car to open her door. Chivalry was alive and well in Tyler, Texas. The restaurant was built in the shape of a big barn with open rafters and red walls. The touch of homeliness did nothing to detract from the city's most sophisticated eating establishment.

Gail ordered a steak and salad with French dressing. Jamison opted for the larger dinner, which included a baked potato. For the first few minutes they ate in relative silence, making only the occasional culinary comment. Jamison was the first to bring up the subject of work.

"Did you bring your list?"

"So, you did mean what you said about this being a business dinner. Yes, I have it right here," she answered, reaching inside her purse. "The 'A' list, right? I started with 'adultery' like you suggested and then went to 'adore.' How about you?"

"Hm…. 'Adore' as in he adores the victim? I don't know. I put 'abandon' as in someone abandoned the killer and this is revenge."

"Interesting idea. Hadn't thought of it that way. My word meant that he adored the girls and wanted to keep them just the way they were so he killed them."

"Ah, I see. Makes sense. What is your next word?"

"I put 'abase', but it really doesn't fit. He didn't abase them, did he?"

"No. I put 'A List.' You know, like the best of the best."

"Weak, Jamison. I expected more."

"This from a woman who had a list of one."

"Ha. Ha. Well, maybe it is his initial."

"Or the initial of someone important to him? You're right. This is useless. Let's go on to something else."

"Let's forget shop for awhile. Tell me something about yourself."

Pagan stared a moment, then threw back her head and laughed. "What am I supposed to do? Try to seduce him? Hang around his office with a copy of his book pretending to be a fan? This is so lame."

Demetri glared at her across the desk. "I appreciate your well-thought out analysis. If I feel I need any more input, I'll be sure to ask."

"So, I am supposed to just offer myself as a sacrifice—no questions asked?"

"It would be nice."

She folded her arms after making a rude gesture in his general direction. "My uncle has agreed to this?"

"No. We are keeping this on a 'need to know basis', and only you and I need to know. Kind of like our other little secret."

She looked at the photograph of the painting of Carl Hardwicke and shivered. How could she look at him face to face, knowing what he did to those girls—knowing what he would do to her if he got the chance? "Fine. Whatever it takes to save my uncle. Do you have a plan or am I just supposed to wing it?"

"We have a lot to discuss, and I'm starved. Let's call it a night. I'll give you a lift and we can pick up something to eat on the way. Okay?"

"Is riding with you and eating with you part of my assignment?"

He lifted an eyebrow in reaction. "If it has to be. I had hoped you might look at this a little differently."

She stood up. "Oh really? You thought I might embrace a blackmail plot involving the possible loss of my life?"

"Thought you might want to help stop a killer. Your job will be to flush him out—not to become one of his rose girls. Come on, let's go."

"Fine. You have it all figured out, don't you?"

"Not everything, not yet. But I will."

She looked into his chestnut-colored eyes wanting to believe he really could protect her. Under different circumstances, she would have found him immensely attractive. Too bad that wasn't the case now. "I think you're an arrogant SOB, who will say or do anything you can to get your man, regardless of the cost. Sure, let's go."

The walk to the Lexus was stiff and awkward. Pagan led the way, leaving Demetri to follow in her wake. He forced her to wait by the passenger side, while he took his time using the keypad to unlock the door. His little show of power only served to increase the enmity between them.

The uneasy stand off continued until they reached the restaurant despite his futile attempts to engage her in conversation. Her folded arms and closed mind challenged him more than he would have liked to admit. Not used to being rebuffed, he found the experience slightly unnerving. But what else could he expect under the circumstances? Not exactly the situation where he could use his charm to its best advantage. But the evening was still young.

Pagan stole a covert glance at Demetri as they pulled into the parking lot. God, he was insufferable. The epitome of everything she detested most about men. Too bad he had to be so damn good looking. How could she control her thoughts when her eyes were sending altogether different signals to her brain? She thought back to their first two encounters. Even then, she knew he was different from the other men in her life. More, somehow. This was proving to be a long night.

Jamison looked at Gail with new eyes. "You want to talk about me? Why? All policemen are basically the same. But you already know that, don't you?"

Her brow furrowed in thought. "No, I don't know that. Listen, if you don't want to talk about yourself, fine. I just wanted to have a break from the case, that's all. I didn't mean to pry."

Jamison was quiet for a minute, seemingly concentrating on his food. When he looked up at Gail, his eyes were thoughtful. "It's been a long day. Guess I'm just a little touchy. I grew up here. Been here all my life. Whole family lives in the area?"

"Are you and your family close?"

"Not very. Not anymore."

"Are your parents still living?"

His eyes narrowed. "Just my mother. We don't talk much anymore, but I still feel close to her. How about you?"

"I grew up in Gladewater. My folks still have a farm there. Came to Tyler to go to college and never left."

"Have any brothers or sisters?"

"One of each. They live in Longview. You? Have any siblings, I mean."

"No, I was the first and the last—an only child."

"Were you lonely growing up?"

He shook his head. "Never thought about it. I had my mother and my friends. I was never really alone."

"But you live alone now, right?"

"Yes, but my mother and I keep in contact, and there's the department."

"The department kind of sums up my life too. Ever thought of getting married and starting a family of your own?"

Jamison took a sip of tea. "Is that your polite way of asking if I'm gay?"

Gail looked surprised. "No, that possibility hadn't actually occurred to me. It's okay if you are, though."

He seemed pleased with her answer. "So open-minded of you. Or is gayness an open challenge to every woman's seductive abilities? But no, I'm not gay. Just haven't found a woman who suited me. How about you?"

"Me? Too busy with my career, I guess. Which brings us back to the subject of the case? What do you think our next move should be?"

"Watch Hardwicke. Wait for him to make a mistake. He will, you know. They all do."

"Does Italian sound all right to you?"

Pagan gave Demetri a hard look. "I'm not hungry. Suit yourself. You seem to be very good at doing that."

Ranoir pulled the car into a parking space without further comment. She was set on being difficult, and he knew nothing he could do or say would change that. He'd seen her type before plenty of times—selfish, egocentric, full of herself and what she wanted, oblivious to the wants and needs of others. There was only one way to handle a woman like that.

He parked the car and started around to open her door. She was out of the car and waiting by the time he reached her. Taking her by the arm, he guided her to the restaurant. At first, she resisted his touch, but as his grip increased, it was either go along or create a public display. She remained compliant until they were seated and the waiter had left for their drink order.

"What in the hell do you think you're doing? I agreed to go undercover, I didn't agree to be manhandled. Don't try that again."

"Or what? You think you can take me, Mallory? This is blackmail. Remember? That means that this is not an agreement—it is a take-over. My game, my rules. You will do what you are told—when you are told. Is that clear?"

"You can't do that," she replied, but her voice was hesitant—less sure.

"I can, and I will. Get used to it. Until this killer is caught, you will answer to me. Tell me you understand."

He watched as she picked up her glass of water and wondered if she had the nerve to toss it in his face. Indecision was etched plainly across her features as she struggled with her desires versus the possible cost. It was with a feeling of relief that he watched her take a drink and set down the glass.

"I think I understand you perfectly," she said. "But just so you understand me. This will all be over one day, and I plan to still be around. So I wouldn't advise you to do anything that you might later have cause to regret. Do you understand me?"

God, she had a lot of spunk. "Is that a threat?"

She smiled. "Oh, I think you know it's much more than that, Agent Ranoir. I think you know exactly what it is."

The rest of the meal passed uneventfully with Pagan picking at her food and only eating what she couldn't resist. Demetri tried to keep a semblance of conversation going, being careful to stay on a non-controversial topic. The topic didn't turn back to the case until almost the end of the meal.

"School begins in another week. I want you to sign up for one of his classes."

Pagan gave herself a moment to think before answering. "Won't that seem strange for a college graduate to sign up for a junior college course?"

"Who would know? Teachers don't bother to check the background of their students."

"And what do I tell my uncle?"

"The truth. Tell him that you are doing some background work for me on the case. He'll accept that."

"Sounds like you've got it all worked out."

"I do," he answered, his voice displaying more confidence than he actually felt.

CHAPTER 13

▼

The body was light and limp, hanging over his arm like a wet towel. He judged she would be out for several more hours. All the others were. This was his special time. He had given them theirs already. Flowers, dinner, dancing—what more could a girl ask for?

He had initially seen her in the park walking her dog—a poodle. He liked girls who liked pets. Showed a nurturing spirit. He began to walk, too—taking care not to get too far ahead of her or too close. Near the end of the walking trail—not too far from his car, he pretended to twist his ankle. No threat there. As he had hoped, she came over immediately to help.

She was tall. About 5'11 and thin. He guessed her to be about 145 lbs. It was, however, her smile he really noticed. She had an easy—always-ready-for-a-laugh smile—as if life were the most pleasant experience in the world. He felt good knowing she would die with that same attitude still intact.

Her hair was brown. Not any special brown, just burnished mahogany hanging in medium-length soft, loose curls that bounced when she walked. That was one of things he had first noticed about her—one of the things he had liked. Mostly, he was a blonde man, but this brunette really caught his eye. Maybe he was changing his tastes. He liked that thought. The idea of change. The idea that he could change.

So, he walked on ahead, paying her no mind and pretended to trip. It wasn't a very graceful execution, but it served its purpose. She ran over immediately to see if he was hurt. By this time he had his ankle firmly in hand. A subtle groan escaped his lips, as if he were trying to hide his pain. A covert glance told him she had noticed his brave efforts and was impressed.

"Do you think it's broken?"

"Oh, no," he said, sounding a little breathless. "It'll be fine. If I could just stand up and walk a little."

She looked skeptical. "I don't know if you should be walking on it. If it's not broken, it's probably sprained."

Her concern was heartwarming. But now came the most difficult part. Could he convince her to help him—have dinner with him? Because for the game to continue, she had to agree of her own free will. It was one of his rules. He chose them, and then they had to choose. If they chose to leave, the game would be over. But if they chose to stay, he would make them immortal.

"You need to have a doctor look at it for you? Are you parked close by?"

"Yes, right over there."

"If you lean on my arm, maybe we can make it to your car." Then suddenly she stopped, as a thought occurred to her. "It's your right foot. You aren't going to be able to drive."

He waited for a minute, letting her think things through, while giving his ankle an occasional rub as a gentle reminder of his pain. She wasn't long in coming to a decision. A man with an injured ankle wasn't very threatening.

"I'll drive you in my car."

He attempted to look gratefully humbled, with just a touch of regret—not a mean feat in itself. One emotion was easy to produce, but the subtle blending of two or more was always tricky. "No, I couldn't. I thank you. I really do, but I wouldn't dream of putting you out of your way."

"Nonsense. It won't be out of my way at all. I wouldn't feel right leaving you like this."

He smiled. "I'm so lucky to find a Good Samaritan in this day and age. They have become so rare. You must be a very special lady."

Her smile told him his comment had found its mark. "Not so rare here. You're in the Bible Belt, you know."

He managed to look surprised. "Am I really? Well, that doesn't make your act any less courageous. I will accept your kind offer, knowing that I will be providing another star for your crown."

That did it. Some days things just seem to go right. In a few minutes they were in her car, talking away like old friends. Dinner was only a short step away. It was all so easy—like the whole thing was a well-rehearsed play, about to raise the curtain on the fourth act.

They stopped at a local EMC where his uninjured leg was expertly wrapped as he groaned appropriately. She had wanted to change clothes when he suggested dinner, but he convinced her otherwise, using his leg once again as his cover.

She chose a tearoom—small and intimate where they could spend some time getting to know one another, for by now they were becoming fast friends. He coaxed her out of her shell with the skill of a master jeweler faceting the perfect diamond from an ungainly lump of crystal. He liked to watch her talk. Her mouth moved back and forth over her food erotically, alternately hiding and revealing the depths inside her. He wondered what it would be like to taste that mouth—later—when she wouldn't object to his doing so.

Large brown eyes studied him in frank approval, never doubting their judgment or insight into human character. Where was that elusive sixth sense when you needed it? He could see that she was sure he was exactly what he seemed to be—safe, reliable, and honorable. Her eyelids fluttered provocatively. She wanted him to be what she saw—willed it—never realizing he willed something entirely different.

Finally, dinner was over and the evening was ready to begin. He leaned against her heavily on the way to the car, using up what little energy she had left. By the time she slid behind the wheel, the drug he had placed into her drink was firmly in control. One minute they were laughing over some inane joke and the next, she was lying witless with her head lolling on the back of the seat. He smoothed her hair away from her face and started the car. Plenty of time to move her later.

Moving to the center of the seat, he eased his left leg over to work the gas and brake pedals, pushing both of her legs as far as possible toward the door. With his left arm supporting her neck, he drove the car with his right. Awkward, but do-able. The backing out was tricky, but after that, the ride was a piece of cake. When he reached the dark alley behind the adjoining shopping strip, he stopped and moved her to the passenger seat. Two blocks later, he secured a dozen red roses from a roadside vendor, not his usual choice. Now, he was set.

With several hours to kill and his prey ready for the taking, he decided to do something new. Something to add to his evening making it more pleasurable, more memorable. Keeping to the back roads, he left the bright lights of the city, letting the glow from the full moon lure him to open fields under the canopy of a starry sky. Not his usual fare, but tonight he felt different—wanting—needy. Always before, he had done it for her, keeping her memory alive through the petals and the blood. Tonight he wanted more.

He drove for miles before he found a place that suited him. Open, pristine in the faded whiteness of the round yellow moon, picturesque with the narrow stream running through the center. He stopped the car and got out. The world stood still as he carried her, weightless in his powerful arms, to the most beautiful spot he could imagine. There, under the light of the golden moon, he worshipped her, loved her—consumed her. And when it was over, he felt satiated—at peace. At least for a while.

The rest was routine and ceremony. A play acted out to appease the demons and to keep the hell-hounds at bay. What was life anyway but a role chosen for us by the gods to nurture their endless perversions? Wasn't his own life proof of that? What else could explain the accidental death of a mother at the hand of her beloved ten-year old son? What else could explain a grief too great to ever be absolved or contained?

He laid the woman on the ground, crossing her arms over her chest in an attitude of death. Soon she would be ready, and the circle would be completed once again. He combed her hair and painted her face from the makeup he found in her purse. She looked like an angel. Finding her complete, he took his knife and cut the artery at the base of her neck. The blood flowed black, pooling behind her like a cloak. He stood up. The rose petals floated from his hands to cover the dying woman in a shroud of crimson perfection. When she was gone, he would cut the "A" into her abdomen, marking her forever as his.

Petals floating
On crimson tide,
Beauty in death
As beauty in life.

The gods mistook you.
Stole from me.
Broke your body
Set you free

Can I do less?
Do I owe more?
Than blood for blood
An even score.

86   Red Red Rose

*   *   *   *

Mallory nursed his second cup of coffee like a lover's last goodbye. "What is it about your coffee that keeps me so addicted, Maria?"

"I stir it with my finger to make it extra sweet. Would you like another cup?"

"What I need is to get to work. What I want is to get a serial killer off the streets."

Maria brought the coffeepot to the table and sat down. "What makes a person into a serial killer, Mr. M.?"

"That is the million dollar question, Maria. All animals, including humans, have an inborn aversion to killing their own species. Even soldiers have to undergo rigorous training to be able to overcome this inhibition. Some never do, even when their own life is endangered."

"So, what happened to these people to make them into killers?"

"Some say heredity, some say environment. Some hypothesize about brain chemicals and extra chromosomes. The truth is no one knows for sure."

"I just don't see what they get out of it," Maria said, shaking her head. "It's almost like they're not human."

"Ah, but therein lies the rub. They are human. Ninety percent of the time, when they aren't killers, they may act as human as you or me. That's what makes them so hard to detect—their normalcy. Now, I definitely need another cup of coffee."

William T. Sundae took one final glance in the mirror before heading outside to make his way down the street to the coffee shop. Gnarled, arthritic fingers straightened a tie, which had seen too many coffee drippings to pass for clean. The cuffs on his gray suit were frayed and brown, but his old eyes didn't see so well anymore and he didn't notice the obvious signs of wear and tear. To him, he looked as dapper as he had in his youth, when the girls swooned at his every sigh and hung on his every word. Billy Boy, they had called him then—in their back-handed whispers and giggled conversations in the locker room. They thought he was cute—the bee's knees—or was that later on. He couldn't remember now. Time shouldn't travel so swiftly or ravage so thoroughly.

The morning was cool, and Billy was glad to have on the full dress suit. Odd weather for this time of year, but it happened sometimes. Bothered his knee a bit. What can you do? Should have taken more care when he was young. Didn't expect to ever get old—not then—not this old. There's Ola Whitcomb sitting out on her porch. Old bag of wind. Crazy old woman thought he'd be game for dinner and a good squeeze. Pashaw on that. He'd had his eye on this thirty-five year old blonde for over a year now. Gonna ask her out too. Just as soon as he got this month's check in the mail.

Two cars came sailing down the road, forcing Billy to the far side next to the curb. Durn women drivers. Not that he really saw the driver's sex, but saying it felt good. He removed his hat, brushing imaginary dirt from the brim before returning it to cover the few whispy hairs lying across the top of his head. The alley would be safer than this and closer too. He hated it though—hated to smell the cans of garbage—hated the stray cats.

Crossing several carefully tended yards, he reached the end of the alley a few minutes later. Rocks and clay. He had gone about fifty feet when a blur of red caught his attention. At first, he ignored it, being used to seeing all manner of things in an alley. But then he noticed something different about this particular item. The cats. Several cats were gathered around the place where the red had appeared, and they didn't scare off—even though he was waving his hat and shooing at them excitedly. He crossed to the side of the alley where the red was laying, even more curious than before.

The red was clearer now. Looked like...he took a few steps closer. Yep, it looked like flowers. A bunch of flowers—red ones—all spread out. He had almost turned away when something else caught his attention. Behind one of the cans was a head. Yeah, now he could see. It was a mannequin. Someone threw away a mannequin and some flowers. Strange that. Wondered if they stole it from one of those department stores. Lots of theft going on nowadays. Not like when he was growing up. He continued his walk to the coffee shop. Back then, you could leave your doors wide open and know your stuff was safe. Course you didn't have much stuff in those days. Not much to look at—not much to steal. He crossed back to the other side of the alley. Wondered if that blonde would go out for a cup of coffee? Sight better her than Ola Whitcomb. Maybe he should give her a call.

CHAPTER 14

▼

Mallory was seated in his office when the call came through.

"They've found another one," Theo said, through his partially opened door, like she didn't have the time to come all the way in. "I have a feeling about this one. They found her in an alley behind some garbage cans."

He joined her in the hall. "The last body was found just off an alley. Let's take my car," he finished, as they headed into the lot.

She nodded, "True, but not around the garbage."

"You think the killer is changing his MO?"

"Not his MO, but it is possible he's changing—evolving." She buckled her seatbelt and waited until he had started the car before continuing. "He started out on a mission. Somewhere along the way he may have decided he enjoyed the crime for its own sake."

"Okay. Say, his motivation does change. How will we be able to tell?"

"Through any number of ways. But if he's changed, we'll know."

"Who found the body?"

"The trash pick-up service. The two men thought it was a mannequin at first, but soon discovered the truth. They were, naturally, quite shaken up. By the time forensics showed up, reporters were already being turned away from the scene. The press has been cooperative and patient, but I have a feeling this whole thing is about to break wide open."

"What effect do you think this will have on the murderer?"

"Too soon to tell. Could make him angry or could propel him into stardom."

"Let's just hope it makes him careless."

Mallory parked the car at the far end of the alley, taking much the same route as Billy Sundae. The bed of red clay forming the makeshift road was traveled by the Department of Sanitation every other day, but allowed few tracks on its hard surface. He looked around. Most of the yards butting up to the alley were enclosed by fences. Some, however, were open, so that it was hard to tell where the alley stopped and the yard began. The killer could have gained access to the alley from any of these yards as well as from the two open ends of the dirt road.

The yard where the body was placed did have a fence—wooden, slatted. One of the woman's shoulders lay directly under the first board with the line of her body angling out toward the alley. He and Theo stared at the body for a long moment without speaking. There was something unsettling about it—something more than the death itself.

"Notice anything different about this one?" asked Chief Redford, coming up beside him.

"Yes, I'm just trying to decide what."

Theo walked closer to the two men. "It's the pose. With a few subtle adjustments to the legs and arms, he has managed to convey the impression of indecency without overtly drawing our attention to the fact. He wanted her to look dirty."

"Why would he do that when he went out of his way to make sure the others didn't?"

Theo cocked her head. "Maybe because of something she was or something she did. Perhaps the autopsy will tell us what it was."

Pagan sat in the registrar's office looking every bit as bored as she was. She could think of at least a dozen better ways to get the low down on Carl Hardwicke than by sitting through his course for three hours every week. What did Ranoir expect him to do? Reveal himself during one of the class lectures? Not bloody likely. She would have to come up with her own plan. If Hardwicke were the killer, she would get the proof needed to convict him. Her thoughts were interrupted when a bouncy blonde coed plopped down beside her on the bench.

"Been waiting long?"

Pagan smiled and tried to act friendly. "Not really. Shouldn't be too much longer."

"How many classes are you taking?"

"Just one."

"I won't have to wait too long then. Hi! My name is Sheila Harold."

"Pagan Mallory."

"What class are you taking, if you don't mind my asking?"

Pagan held out her course sheet. "Hardwicke's poetry course. Supposed to be really good."

"Oh yeah? I need another elective. I might just take that, too. Is it a two or three day class? Morning or afternoon?"

"The course schedule showed it being offered several different times. I'm taking it M-W-F at nine o'clock."

Sheila opened her notebook. "Hey, that would work for me. I'll try to get in the same class."

A stern looking matron appeared in the doorway, nodding in their direction. "Pagan Mallory?" she asked, making the name sound like a reprimand.

With a half wave in Sheila's direction, Pagan stood and followed the woman into the adjoining office to officially become enrolled in the junior college.

Debbie Patten's photographs were hung beside the pictures of the other four victims forming a kind of rose parade of death across the south wall of Mallory's office. He stared at them in turn, willing them to give him the information he lacked, information that would lead to the identity of their killer.

A knock on the door interrupted his thoughts. Theo joined him at the wall, her hands folded behind her clasping a manila folder. "It's too macabre, isn't it? Did we ever find out anything on where he got the roses?"

"The florists we contacted told us that they weren't part of their stock. They further stated that the flowers he used were either home grown or bought on a local street corner."

"A lot of good that will do us."

"It might. Roses don't stay in season all year. Soon, he will either have to change flowers or purchase them at a very high cost and become visible."

"Might he grow them in a hot house?"

"He might, but then again, he is strengthening his exposure. Have you gotten the autopsy report?"

She sat down in one of the chairs sitting in front of his desk. "This attack was different," she said, laying the folder on the desk. "First of all, the girl was drugged. We found flunitrazepam in her blood stream."

"Does this drug have a more common name?"

"Yes, I'm sorry. You are probably more familiar with it as Rohypnol."

"The date-rape drug?"

"That's the one. People who have ingested Rohypnol, particularly when coupled with alcohol, will have very little, or no recall of events that have transpired.

Sedation occurs twenty to thirty minutes after ingestion, having its peak effect within one to two hours. Sedation lasts for eight hours after two milligrams are ingested. Symptoms include drowsiness, impaired motor skills, impaired judgment, disinhibition, dizziness, confusion, and amnesia."

"And did he rape her?"

"There's no trace of sperm, but physical indications are that he did."

"But we still don't have any DNA?"

Theo smiled. "Actually, we do. We have a couple of hairs that did not belong to the victim. We're running them now against the national data bank."

"So, unless he's been cited for a prior offense, we won't find a match."

"Exactly, but chances are good that he has."

"Anything else?"

"The dump site was different. The work was sloppy, and the stomach contents were specific to an area tearoom. Do you remember the last lines of the poem he left?

Can I do less?

Do I owe more?

Than blood for blood

An even score.

His mission has undergone a subtle change. Instead of talking about worship and an act of love, he is now writing about revenge. Revenge involving violence."

Mallory rubbed his forehead—a telltale sign of stress. "Do you have any good news to share?"

She smiled sympathetically. "Well, violence is sloppy and messy. Mistakes will be easy to make and hard to cover up. Our chance of catching him increases."

By the time the yellow Karmann Ghia turned the corner into the driveway, Pagan was ready for a break, and she knew just what to do. Grabbing a slip of paper off her dresser she picked up the phone and dialed Chad DeForest, the cowboy turned preppie. Just the man she needed to give her a new lease on life.

"Hello."

"May I speak to Chad DeForest, please?"

"Speaking."

"Oh. Well, this is Pagan Mallory. We ran into each other at the convenience store and…"

"I remember you, Pagan. How have you been?"

92   Red Red Rose

"In need of a break. You got plans for tonight?"

"Now, I do. What did you have in mind?"

"Whatever. Little dinner, little dancing, little fruit of the vine," she said, twirling her hair through her fingers like she did when she was five.

"Give me your address, and I'll pick you up about seven."

"Do I need to locate a ladder?"

"A ladder? Oh, I see. My monster truck made quite an impression on you. Actually, I was planning to bring my car. If that's all right?"

"Sure, fine. Got a pen?"

After she'd given her address and hung up, she threw herself on the bed with an immense feeling of relief. How do guys do that all the time? Glad to be of the female persuasion. Two hours, one long bath, and half a closet of discarded clothes later, she was dressed. Maria was waiting for her when she descended the stairs.

"You look too good for the boys around here, Missy. Turn around and let me see you."

Pagan twirled around obediently, just as she had when she was in grade school and let Maria fuss over her. "Like my hair back like this or should I take it down?"

"You look very grown up and sophisticated. I like it up."

"Thanks Maria," she said, giving her a quick hug as the doorbell sounded. "Right on time. Talk to you when I get back. Don't wait up."

Pagan took a quick look out the peek hole and opened the door without hesitation. "Hey. You want to come in?"

He shrugged. All six foot, five inches of him. "Got a table waiting at Johnny's, but it's up to you."

Pagan grinned. "I never keep seafood waiting. See you later, Maria," she said, pulling the door closed behind her. As he walked her to the black Jaguar, she could not help but notice how very fine he looked. Preppie again for sure. Must have realized how much she liked it.

On the way to the restaurant he told her about his work in computers. She was dutifully impressed and managed to avoid answering questions about her own interests except on the most superficial level. He was fun, interesting, but not entertaining enough to keep her mind off her job and what role she had been ordered to play.

Dinner was delicious, culminating in a large heap of Alaskan king crab claws dripping in butter. Eating took precedent over conversation until the meal was almost over. Toward the end he suggested they go to the Red Rose. Pagan readily agreed, hoping the lighter atmosphere would make her date a little more fun. It was at the club that things began to pick up.

Chad guided her up to the bar with confidence. Not a big drinker, Pagan ordered a wine cooler, from which she took an occasional sip. Chad, however, started with a shot of Tequila that he knocked back without effort. Almost immediately he began to change. All the formality that had kept him at arm's length during dinner was gone. He was friendly, funny, life of the party. She began to relax. This guy was really great—someone she might like to have a real relationship with. They danced for over an hour.

At about eleven o'clock they sat down at a table to take a break. Chad was in a great mood laughing and cracking jokes. He brought fresh drinks to the table and pulled his chair close. He smelled good, and she realized how much she had missed having a regular guy to hang out with. Since her uncle had moved to East Texas, she had enjoyed very little in the way of a social life. When they had finished their drinks, Chad suggested they leave.

She was surprised to find she could barely stand, much less walk to the car. Chad didn't seem to mind. He just swooped her into his arms and carried her. Once in the car, she fell back in the seat—half awake, half asleep. By the time Chad slipped in next to her, she was almost asleep. Not even his slow kisses could wake her up.

The next thing she became aware of was men shouting somewhere around her and the violent slamming of car doors. She tried to open her eyes, but they were heavy. The yelling seemed to go on for some time before her door was opened and she was moved to a different place. After that everything went black. That was the last thing she would remember until morning.

CHAPTER 15

▼

Streams of muted sunlight filtered through the bedroom window. Pagan threw her arm across her face to shield her eyes, but that wasn't what had awakened her. The constant whispering was what had brought her to consciousness. Peeking from under the curve in her arm, she saw Maria sitting in the corner of her room reciting the rosary, her eyes red from crying. Pagan sat up immediately.

"Maria, what's wrong? Has something happened to Uncle Mal? What's going on?"

Maria ran to the bed and threw her arms around her dramatically, muttering all the while in unintelligible Spanish. Pagan felt a knot of fear form in the pit of her stomach. She was well on the way toward blind panic when with a soft knock on the bedroom door, her uncle came into the room. She set Maria gently aside.

"Would someone please tell me what is going on?"

Mallory pulled a chair up beside the bed. "What do you remember about last night, Pagan?"

Confusion settled her face into tight lines. "Last night? Why is that important? Chad took me out to eat, and then we went to the Red Rose to dance. I don't remember much after that. I think I fell asleep. Why? What's happened?"

She had seldom seen her uncle look more serious. "Are you familiar with the drug Rohypnol?"

She scrunched up her face. "Isn't that the date-rape drug?"

"Yes. Seems you ingested a substantial amount last night."

Pagan shook her head. "No, I didn't. I was with Chad. What is this all about?"

Maria made a blubbering noise, which earned her an immediate look of censure from Mallory.

- 94 -

"How much did you have to drink last night with Chad?"

"A couple of wine coolers."

"Do wine coolers usually make you pass out?"

Pagan was becoming irritated. "I didn't pass out, Uncle Mal. I was just sleepy. I fell asleep. Why are you making such a big deal out of this?"

"Do you remember the sirens and the police cars? Do you remember being driven home in a police car? Do you remember being carried to your room or the doctor examining you? Do you remember Maria dressing you for bed?"

Pagan sat still for a long time. "Did he rape me?"

"No. We got there in time. He's in jail."

She dropped her head into her hands. "How did you know?" She looked up when her uncle failed to answer. "How did you know to come?" she repeated.

"Demetri made the call."

"Demetri," she gasped, spitting out the word—a foreign object that had become lodged in her throat. "What does he have to do with all this?"

Mallory made a coughing sound. "Seems he had you under surveillance."

"He was watching me?"

"No, he had you bugged."

"Bugged? How?"

Mallory had the grace to look embarrassed. "Your watch. The bug is implanted in your watch."

She looked down as he was talking. Then, tearing it off her wrist, she threw the watch enthusiastically across the room, watching as it slammed against the wall. After a minute she faced her uncle. "Did you know about this?"

"No."

"So what is the charge against Chad? Attempted rape?"

"For now. And possession and use of the Rohypnol."

"What do you mean, 'for now?'" Are you going to charge him with something else?"

Mallory cleared his throat. "We got the autopsy back on the last victim. She had been given Rohypnol and raped before her death."

The horror of his implication was mirrored on her face. "But surely you don't think Chat was capable of committing the *Rose* murders?"

"He is apparently capable of committing rape. Someone who looks and acts normal is capable, otherwise we would have spotted him by now."

"Where is Agent Ranoir right now?"

"Downstairs. He wants to ask you some questions about last night."

Pagan's head snapped up at that. "That's fine, because I have some questions of my own to ask."

Pagan dressed quickly, seemingly unharmed by her ordeal until she saw last night's torn blouse in the bottom of the trash. The physical reminder seemed to bring it all back, and she swayed slightly on her feet.

Maria reached out to balance her. "You need to rest. Lay down. I'll bring you something to eat."

"I'm fine, really. Just a little off balance from all that's happened. It feels so bizarre to know something so dramatic happened to me, and I can't remember it. I'll eat something downstairs in a few minutes, but right now I want to take a shower and dress."

"I understand. Go ahead, and I'll be here if you need me."

"Thank you, Maria," she said, giving her a big hug.

Pagan opened the water faucet in the shower and stepped inside. The warm stream felt good. For a while she just stood, letting the soothing spray wash away any thoughts of Chad and what he had tried to do. Later would be time enough to analyze what had happened and why. Right now, she just wanted to relax.

By the time she started downstairs, she felt fresh and ready for a much-needed confrontation. She found Demetri in the kitchen with Maria, enjoying his second cup of coffee.

"You wanted to see me?" she said, immediately alerting him to her frame of mind.

"Yes, but my questions can wait until after you've eaten."

"Really? How thoughtful of you. Well, mine can't. I want you to explain to me exactly how you knew I was in trouble."

If the task left him uncomfortable, he didn't show it. "I planted a listening device in your watch."

"Why? Am I a suspect in the *Rose* murders?"

"No, of course not."

"Then, why?"

He hesitated and looked toward Maria. "We need to talk about this later."

She followed his look. "Maria, could you excuse us for just a minute?"

Wiping her hands on her apron, Maria gave Demetri a cold look and left the room.

"Okay, we're alone. Now, answer the question."

He gave her a sheepish look. "I knew you were going to register at the college and was worried about you running into Hardwicke."

Pagan sat back in her chair. "Wasn't that the idea? Isn't that why I am taking the course?"

He nodded. "Yes, but I had wanted to prepare you first."

"Prepare me how?"

"Issue you a weapon."

Pagan lifted her eyebrows in surprise. "You mean a gun? You want me to carry a gun?"

"Yes. Do you know how to shoot?"

"Not really. I'm not sure I'll feel comfortable with a gun," she said, not confessing that she had already been planning on buying one. She liked this show of protectiveness, even if it was just for the sake of the investigation.

"In that case, you're in the wrong line of work. Being a detective can be dangerous work. You need a gun, and you need to know how to use it. After breakfast we'll make a visit to the local gun shop and the firing range. I don't want you out there unprotected."

Pagan brought Maria back into the room. "Sorry about that. Agent Ranoir views his whole life as a secret mission. It's best if we just humor him."

He shot her a dirty look, then turned his attention to Maria's western omelet. It was good. Pagan was surprised at the strength of her appetite. Twenty minutes later they were on the road.

Mallory reviewed DeForest's file for the third time. No priors—clean sheet. Could this man possibly be the killer? Somehow, he doubted it. Anyone with a five-dollar bill could score roche. DeForest had some on him when they had picked him up, which along with the attempted rape was worth a felony conviction. The DNA test would be in shortly. If his DNA matched the evidence taken from the last murder victim, they would have a strong case. If not, they would only have the drug link. He connected with Jenkins on the in-house phone.

"Jenkins? Mallory. I'm going out for a while. Patch through to me if anything important turns up."

The traffic was mild for midday. Tyler had long ago outgrown its transportation layout on the South side, and construction work had been underway for over a year. The Lotus Tearoom was the only restaurant in the city serving all three of the ingredients found in the stomach of the fifth victim, Debbie Patten. Having a distinct Oriental flavor set them apart from other tearooms in the city. A picture of Patten had been obtained yesterday when police had searched her apartment. She had been an attractive woman. Now, to see if anyone recognized her.

98   Red Red Rose

Mallory was shown to a table by a woman who didn't look or sound as if she spoke much English. It was a possibility he had not anticipated. He was therefore relieved when the waitress arrived and was obviously local.

"What would you like to drink?" she asked, in a rather broad twang.

"Iced tea would be fine," he answered, pulling out his badge. The girl was taken aback. "I really need your help."

She looked skeptical. "What do you need?"

"This girl came here to eat yesterday. Do you remember seeing her?"

She looked at the picture. "Yes, I think she ate over there at table three. Just a minute I'll ask Susan. She works that section."

A few minutes later she returned with another girl. "This is Susan. She remembers her."

"Hello, Susan. I'm Police Chief Detective Mallory. You served this girl yesterday?"

She wiped her hands nervously on her apron. "Yes. Is something wrong?"

"Was she alone?"

"No, she was with a man. I remember because he had a hurt foot, and he leaned on her to walk."

"Could you describe the man for me? This could be very important."

"I didn't pay a lot of attention. He had brown hair and looked athletic. Maybe because he was wearing a jogging suit and jogging shoes. She was, too. Dressed to go jogging, I mean."

"You said his foot was hurt?"

"Yeah, it had been bandaged up."

"Like a hospital bandage or something done at home?"

"Like at a hospital."

"Do you remember anything else?"

"No, not really."

Mallory pulled out one of his cards. "If you think of anything, please call me at this number. I may send over a sketch artist later to get a description from you. Would you check around and see if anyone remembers anything else?"

"Sure," she said, eyeing his ten-dollar tip.

Mallory thanked her and left.

The morning newspaper lay rolled on the front seat of the car. He had wanted to wait until he was ensconced in the sanctuary of his home before opening it. News of the murders had been broadcast in bits and pieces over the local television and radio stations all day. He knew the newspaper was running the story on the front page as a full-length feature. All five victims would be listed with pictures and biographical information. There was even talk the story would be picked up by the national and international press.

Excitement ran through him like an electrical bolt, making him feel more alive than he ever had before. His work, the story of his creations, was being published for everyone to see. Parental pride bubbled up from somewhere deep within him. He wished she could be here to see his accomplishment—his victory.

The noon sun highlighted the widow's walk while casting the rest of the gray walls in shadow, not unlike a set for a Dracula movie. While in direct opposition, vines of wild roses covered the trellis arches bordering the porch in a riot of bright color. He smiled at the warm memories they always evoked.

Parking the car under the old shed, he entered through the side door without bothering to use the inside lights. The only place to read this paper was in his room, the one he had lived in when she was alive. He opened the door to look on the cherished reminders of his childhood and of his nightmares.

Cars were the theme of his room, beginning with the blue car-bed, and extending to the red car-shaped shelf over his bed, which held his collection of Hot Wheels. Pictures of antique cars in various colors and sizes decorated his window curtain and re-appeared in the throw rugs covering the wood-planked floor.

Plopping down on the bed, much as he had as a child, he opened the paper to the front page. There he saw the headline: "POLICE SEEK SUSPECT IN THE ROSE MURDERS."

Wow! The *Rose Murders*. They had an official name. A title for his work. Skipping the detailed accounts of the murders, he scanned down to the part about the suspects. Some local psychiatrist had provided a profile of the killer, including speculation concerning physical abuse and an unhappy childhood. The doctor couldn't be more wrong. Clearly, people didn't have a clue about what was happening. Maybe he should drop them some hints. He would consider it.

Philistines, all of them. His poetry should have told them all they needed to know. Maybe he was dealing with the wrong people. He turned the page and scanned down. Just as he had suspected, the paper contained none of his poems. Didn't they know poetry was written to be read? Why would they withhold his art? They wouldn't. Of course, that was it. They hadn't withheld it. They had just never received it. An oversight that would be easy to remedy.

Going to the desk in the corner of his room, he extracted several sheets of white paper and began to write. No. Bad idea. They must be typed, like the others. He must remember to stay cool and not get excited. Hasty people made mistakes, and mistakes could prove to be fatal. He must think this through. After all, time was his friend, not theirs.

What to do. People would want to know about him—would want to understand the beauty of what he was doing. Death wasn't at all what most people thought or believed, and people in this part of the country were the worst. They thought their God would save them. That if they were good, they wouldn't suffer. He would prove that to be a fallacy. Hadn't he done so already? He needed a plan, and then he would be ready to act.

CHAPTER 16

▼

Jamison paced up and down the small hall, his mind centered on the prisoner about to be interrogated in the next room. "I want to talk to this guy before he's released. I can get him to talk. He's our guy. I can feel it."

Gail Whiting watched him with growing apprehension. "You'll get your chance, Jamison. Just relax."

"How can you be so calm, Whiting? It could have been you instead of Pagan he drugged and tried to rape."

She stood up. "How dare you? You think I don't want him as bad as you do. I just know Redford is only going to do a preliminary, and since Mallory is too close to the case, you are the next logical person to put in charge of the investigation."

He paused. "Yeah, you're probably right."

"I know I'm right. Let's see if Redford gets anywhere. He's about to go in."

They both watched through the two-way mirror as Redford entered the room and took his seat. Gail turned up the speaker. The first few minutes were taken up with preliminary introductions and explanations to make sure all "i's" were dotted and all "t's" were crossed. DeForest waived his right to have an attorney present.

"Mr. DeForest, is it true you drove Miss Pagan Mallory to a local club called the Red Rose last night?"

"Yes."

"And is it true you bought Miss Mallory two wine coolers during the course of the evening?"

"I don't remember how many she drank, but I think it was two or more."

- 101 -

"Isn't it true you drugged Miss Mallory's drink with Rohypnol, also known as the date-rape drug?"

"No, that is not true."

"Mr. DeForest, Miss Mallory was examined at the end of the evening by a physician and her body was found to contain a significant amount of Rohypnol. At the time of your arrest, you were found with two Rohypnol tablets in your shirt pocket. Do you have any explanation for this seeming coincidence?"

"No, I don't. Anyone could have planted that on me."

"But you were the one found groping a semiconscious Pagan Mallory in your car, were you not?"

"She was a little tipsy, that's all. She wanted me."

"She didn't even know you were there, Mr. DeForest."

Chief Redford stood up and left the room. In a couple of seconds the door opened into the corridor where Whiting and Jamison were waiting. "Jamison, I know you're dying to get in there. I'm sending Whiting in with you. Keep it cool. Keep it professional. He's a wealthy kid with a lot of legal power behind him. We can't afford to lose him over a police brutality charge."

"Yes, sir," both Whiting and Jamison answered.

For the next fifteen minutes Jamison grilled DeForest objectively about the previous evening. After that, the questions became personal. Jamison alternately threatened and taunted DeForest, looking for a slip. He didn't have long to wait.

"Women don't like you, do they DeForest?"

"Women love me. I can get anyone I want."

"If that were true, you wouldn't have to resort to rape, now, would you?"

"I don't rape women."

"You don't stop when they tell you 'no.'"

"I do when they mean it."

"And how can you tell when they don't?"

"A guy can just tell. A lot of women say 'no' when they don't mean it."

"Why would they do that?"

DeForest leaned back in his chair. "Lots of reasons. You have to know women."

"Know them how? Explain."

"Well, most women won't admit it but they like a man who is willing to take charge. When they say 'no' it's like a test to see if a man can do what they really want."

"And what would that be?"

"To be dominated. Women long to be dominated—to be taken. That's what they really want. And afterwards, they're glad."

"And is that what Pagan Mallory wanted?"

"She's a woman, isn't she?"

"And how about Debbie Patten? Is that what she wanted, too?"

DeForest sat forward. "What are you talking about? I don't know a Debbie Patten."

"Sure, you do. She was one of the women who wanted to be dominated."

"Not by me. I never met a woman named Debbie Patten."

Jamison picked up a photograph that was face down on the table and held it up. "Maybe this will refresh your memory."

"She's pretty, but I don't know her."

"Well, maybe you don't remember her because last time you saw her she looked like this." Jamison held up a picture of Patten taken at the crime scene.

"No. No way. You're not gonna pin this on me. I never saw that girl before. No. Get me my lawyer. I want my lawyer."

Pagan looked at Demetri Ranoir's profile from across the car. "What gave you the right to plant a bug on me? Doesn't that violate some civil rights law somewhere?"

They had spent the morning picking out a firearm and using it at the practice range. Pagan proved to be a surprisingly good shot for a beginner.

"I can't believe you're harping on this after I saved you from being raped. Or wouldn't that have violated your civil rights?"

"But you didn't know I was in danger of being raped."

"I knew you were going to be near or with our prime suspect in the case, Carl Hardwicke. I knew you didn't have proper protection. I felt that a little surveillance was the least I could do."

"Oh, I see now. You were feeling guilty for leaving me out in the cold as bait for a serial killer. Mighty thoughtful of you, Ranoir."

"Like I said, it was the least I could do."

Pagan didn't say anything for a minute. "Where are you from originally?"

He turned his head in her direction. "What brought that up?"

"Nothing really. Just curious."

"Where do you think I'm from?"

"Hm…. Some big city where things are impersonal and manners are nonexistent." She was rewarded with one of his infrequent smiles.

"Actually, I grew up on a farm not too far from here."

"No way."

"Ever hear of East Mountain?"

"No."

"Well, my family were farmers. Poor, but proud. You know the type. As soon as I turned eighteen, I left for college and never looked back."

Pagan laughed.

"What do you find so amusing?"

"Nothing really. I'm just having a hard time picturing you 'poor but proud.'"

"Oh, really. Well, we actually had it pretty good. I had an uncle who still used an outhouse. I went to stay with him one time. It was like time traveling. Drawing water from a well, washing clothes out of doors, the outhouse. I decided then and there I was going to get an education and do better."

"So, I guess your uncle didn't have a television either."

He gave her a dour look. "For fun, my cousins and I played 'Annie Over.'"

"Okay, I'll bite. What was 'Annie Over.'"

"That's where you threw a ball over the house, yelling 'Annie Over' then raced around the house to try to catch it."

"Interesting game, Ranoir. I can see why you left at the earliest opportunity."

"Don't knock it until you've tried it."

"And did you play marbles too?"

"Of course. I still have mine—over three hundred and fifty."

"Quite the little collector. I'm impressed. What else did you collect?"

"Would you believe Superman Comic Books?"

"Oh no. I can just see you now in your blue suit and red cape. Your mother made you one to play in, right? And next you're going to tell me about the time you jumped off the roof to fly. Right?"

"No, I didn't go that far. Besides, I didn't jump off things to fly. I just ran really fast and held out my arms until I lifted off the ground."

"So tell me how you went from being a nearly normal child to an FBI agent. Is that as close to being a Superman as you could get in this life?"

He didn't answer, but after the look she got, he didn't have to. So this wasn't an ordinary lawman she was dealing with but one who saw in black and white— right and wrong—good and evil. And in his opinion she had crossed the line and broken the law.

Pagan and Demetri arrived at the police station right after Jamison had finished questioning DeForest. They slipped in through the side door to avoid the questions, the sympathetic looks, and the kind words she knew would be forth-coming.

"Are you sure you want to do this?" Demetri asked, giving her one last chance to back out.

"I'm sure."

"Then leave your weapon with me."

She looked at him in surprise. "Do you think I would try to kill him?"

His raised eyebrows were his only comment, but she got the message.

DeForest had been returned to his cell. He stood as they approached. "I don't want to see her. Guard. Hey, guard. I don't want see her. Don't let her in."

The guard ignored him and opened the door, so DeForest turned his anger to Pagan. "What the hell do you want, bitch? Haven't you done enough already? I'm behind bars. What more do you want?"

She didn't say anything, just walked toward him. When she got close she pretended to trip, and as she fell, raised her knee to strike him hard in the groin. He fell to his knees, doubled over in pain. Before she could do anything more, Ranoir grabbed her by the arms from behind and forced her toward the door.

"Get the nurse," he said to the guard on the way out. "Mr. DeForest has had an accident." Once outside he turned to Pagan. "What in the hell did you think you were doing back there?"

"Just giving him something to remember me by. It was the least I could do."

The anger evident in his face warned her that this time she might have gone too far. She moved to take a step back but his hand shot out to stop her.

She tried to twist away. "Let me go. That hurts."

"You acted like a spoiled brat. We are supposed to uphold the law, not break it."

Her eyes flashed. "You need to lighten up."

"And you need to be spanked."

His words took them both by surprise, and he loosened his grip on her arm. She stepped back, wondering why she felt so intimidated. They stared at each other a moment before he broke the silence.

"Don't look at me like that. I'm not going to hit you."

"Ah, shucks. And I was so looking forward to it," she answered, giving a saucy toss of her head.

"Don't press your luck," he warned, in a low voice. "You might get more than you bargained for."

Jamison opened the door to Jaffie's Bar and Grill with only one thought in mind. He had just downed his first whiskey and water when Whiting joined him at the bar.

"Trying to drown your sorrows."

He looked in her general direction without bothering to turn his head. "Just trying to get some peace. Are you following me?"

"Not really. Was in the mood for a drink myself and saw you walk in. Thought you could use some company."

"What is it with you Whiting? Are you some sort of do-gooder or do you just like to hang out with losers?"

Gail motioned the bartender over. "I'm not sure I know what you mean. I certainly don't consider myself a do-gooder, as you call it."

"Always happy, always cheery. What are you really about, Whiting?"

She shrugged. "Same thing you are, I guess."

His laugh was bitter. "You don't have a clue what I'm about, woman. Not a clue."

"Then why don't you tell me?"

"I asked you first."

She took a long drink. "Well, my life is about police work. Pretty boring by today's standards, I know, but the work is what gives me a sense of meaning. Some day I'd like to have a family, I guess. I really haven't thought too much about that side of things. Now, it's your turn."

"All right, if you want to put it on that note, I guess that my life is about justice."

"Well, you know what they say, 'Justice is blind.'"

"Is that what they say? Well, maybe I figure to be her seeing-eye dog. Maybe that's what police work is all about."

"I don't know, Jamison. I always thought police work was about upholding the law."

He laughed. "And what about guys like Hardwicke and DeForest? One of them is a killer and the other is a rapist—a seducer of women, young women. What about their law?"

"No one promised it would be easy, Jimmy. All we can do is all we can do. That is the most that we can ask of ourselves."

He turned to her and smiled. "Well, at least, we can agree on something."

Pagan and Demetri got into his car without speaking any further about the incident. The ride home was long and tense. This time she was the one who broke the silence.

"All right, I was wrong to do what I did. But can you blame me?"

"That's not the point. We have to be better than base impulse. If he charges police brutality and can make it stick, it might queer the entire case. Do you want to see him go free for what he did or worse—sue the station and collect damages?"

"Fine. I get it. I'm a hotheaded screw-up and the police would do better without me. I quit."

He laughed. "I bet you're really good at that. Too bad you don't have that option."

"What do you mean?"

"How soon they forget? Unless you want your uncle off the case too, you'll continue to do your job and do it well."

She looked out the window. "Why do you still want me?"

"I told you before. I want you as bait. I want you to go to Hardwicke's office, talk to him about the course, tell him how much you admire his work—do whatever it takes to make him notice you. Get him to ask you out. We don't have time to wait for him to see you in class. Get his attention."

"Are you ordering me to sleep with him?"

"I didn't say that. What I said was to go out on a date. Set that up, and then, we'll lay our trap. You'll be wearing a wire, and we'll be well within reach if anything should happen. Just don't drink any alcohol."

"Not that I had planned to, but why not?"

"The chance of him drugging you without it are slim. The date-rape drugs usually depend on the alcohol to help them work. Think you can handle that?"

She gave him a derisive look. "You just be ready to protect me when I'm out with this monster."

The car was too dark for her to see his slow smile.

CHAPTER 17

▼

Theo passed the door to Mallory's office on the way to her own. She had no doubt he was spending another late night going over the facts of the case just as she was. Something was gnawing at her and wouldn't quit. She had the gut feeling they were missing something—something important.

She had been working for about an hour when she was interrupted by the ringing of the phone. The call had come through on her private line.

"Hello."

"Is this Theodora Van Zandt?"

"Yes. May I help you?"

"Maybe. I need someone to give me some advice."

"Who is this?"

A low chuckle followed her question. "Well, let's just say I have a great fondness for red roses, shall we?"

Theo felt as if the wind had been knocked out of her, and for a moment, she couldn't get her breath. What should she do? She was totally unprepared for this kind of a communication. No recording device. No way to call out to anyone. She looked toward the door.

"All right," she said, standing to her feet as quietly as possible. "What can I help you with?" She pulled the cord over to where she could reach the door. Opening it quietly to a point where she could see Mallory's door down the hall, she removed one of her shoes and gave it a hard throw. The second it left her hand she covered the receiver to muffle the sound. The man didn't seem to notice.

"First, I want my poems printed in the press. If you don't, I will. Second, I want you to explain to everyone that this is not murder, and I am not a serial killer. This is art. I resent being referred to as a killer. I create beauty through sacrifice. Do you understand?"

She watched as Mallory opened his door and bent to pick up the shoe. She waved frantically and pointed to the telephone. "Of course, I understand. I realized what you were doing immediately. Art is a form of higher communication and self expression, but I don't know if the police will allow me to release your poetry." By this time Mallory had set up a trace and a recording. Keep him talking his gestures said. She nodded.

"That wouldn't be very wise of them. If I have to send in the poems myself, things might not be so pleasant."

"What do you mean?"

"I mean I might think the police weren't taking me and my art seriously. That would cause me great suffering. And I don't like to suffer alone. Know what I mean?"

"Yes, I think I do. Are there any other ways I could help you? Maybe we could talk about why you feel the need to include murder in your art."

"You'd like that, wouldn't you? But I know you're running a trace on this line. This is all for now. Maybe I'll call you again."

Theo heard the click right before the line disconnected. She put down the receiver and ran out into the hall. "Did we get it?"

Mallory pushed the button to activate the speakerphone and placed an in-house call. "Jenkins, what did you find out."

"We've got a problem, sir. We came up with all but the last number of the call."

"Okay, then, let's use zero through nine for the last number and list the locations of those possible numbers."

The officer cleared his throat. "Well, that's where the problem lies, sir."

"What do you mean?"

There was a slight pause at the other end of the line. "I know this sounds crazy, but using those numbers traces the call to inside the station."

"Re-check it, Jenkins. If it still comes out the same, I want every room checked and dusted for prints, especially the phones. I, also, want a list of the duty roster for tonight and the log of everyone that came in and went out. Also, you better put on a fresh pot of coffee."

Theo joined him in his office. "I'm sorry. The call just took me so completely by surprise."

110   Red Red Rose

Mallory smiled reassuringly. "You did fine. The shoe was inspired. We'll be set up next time. Try to tell me everything you remember he said."

She repeated the conversation while he made notes. After she had finished, he asked more questions.

"I know he talked through a device, but was there anything about his choice of words or his inflection that sounded familiar?"

She thought for a minute. "No, I can't think of anything. Sorry I'm not more help."

"You're doing fine. If you think of anything else, write it down and let me know."

"What does the result of the trace mean? How did he manage to get in?"

"Maybe he just walked in."

"What do you mean? You're not saying he's one of us, are you?"

Mallory sighed. "Right now, we can't afford to rule anything out. Maybe he works here as a custodian or does maintenance repairs."

Theo wasn't buying it. "But if he does work here, why would he give himself away like that? It doesn't make sense."

"No, it doesn't. I'm going to call Ranoir in—see if he has any ideas."

Demetri dropped Pagan off and went straight to his apartment. The long hours and consistent lack of results were beginning to get to him in a big way. He grabbed a beer from the refrigerator and sat down to relax. He reached for the remote and then, stopped. The last thing he wanted to see was more news about the case. If he could just forget it for a few hours, he might have a chance to get some rest.

Before the thought was completely out of his head, the phone rang. No. He wouldn't answer it. He would just let it ring. Four, five, six. Damn. Might as well get it. Knowing Mallory, he would put out an APB. "Hello."

"Ranoir? Mallory. We need you back at the station. There's been a new development."

Ranoir frowned. "I'm on my way." He poured the remainder of the beer down the sink, throwing the can enthusiastically at the trash receptacle. Would this day ever end?

He arrived back at the station in fifteen minutes. Jenkins met him at the door. "Mallory is waiting for you in his office. Don't touch anything. Forensics is down, and we are treating the entire station as a crime scene."

"What in the hell is going on?" he asked, entering Mallory's office.

Mallory motioned him to a chair. "We've had a call from the killer. He called Theo."

Ranoir looked at Theo. "But that doesn't explain about the station—unless…. Tell me I'm wrong. You're not going to say he telephoned you from the station, are you?"

Theo nodded. "The trace puts him here."

"The trace. He talked long enough for a trace. He wants us to know he was here—how clever he is."

"What did he say?"

"He wants us to publish his poems in the paper."

"Why?"

"Says it's his art—it defines his creation."

"What do you make of this guy?"

"Very egotistical. Likes the attention. May not have known that before today. Now, he'll be more unstoppable than ever."

Pagan refused Maria's offer of warm milk and headed to the comfort of her bed. Seems like morning was eons ago. She was tired and drained. Throwing herself across the mattress, she closed her eyes and dozed off to sleep. When she woke up, the sun was bright, and Maria was shaking her excitedly.

"The police are giving interviews on television. That FBI man is about to make a statement." She turned on Pagan's television. Sure enough, there he was, Demetri Ranoir. Maria turned up the sound.

"Yes, it is true. We did receive a call from the man we believe to be the rose killer. That's all I have to say right now. Anything else would put the integrity of the case in jeopardy. We'll be posting updates as new information is available."

Pagan jumped off the bed, wide-awake. "What time is it, Maria?"

"Seven-fifteen."

"Has Uncle Mal even been home, yet?"

"No, he hasn't called, either. Not like him."

"Make me a pot of coffee, Maria. Strong coffee. I'm going to pop in the shower, and then I'll be down."

"Coming right up. Have you a couple of pieces of toast ready too?"

Pagan showered and dressed in record time. She couldn't wait to get to the station.

"Phone call," Maria yelled as she topped the stairs.

Pagan picked the receiver with feelings of apprehension. "Hello?"

"Glad I caught you. Don't come down to the station today, Pagan," Demetri's voice ordered over the phone lines.

"And why not? I want to know what's going on. Maybe I can help. I am supposed to be part of the team."

"Yes, I knew you'd feel that way, but this is different. I don't want to discuss it over the phone. Meet me for breakfast at IHOP in an hour. Okay? I'll explain everything."

She rolled her eyes, not trusting him for a minute. This was just another ploy designed to sideline her. "Fine," she said aloud. "I'll be waiting at the restaurant." Like what choice did she have?

Carl Hardwicke sat in his office looking over his class list for the fourth time. Could it be a coincidence that Pagan Mallory was listed in one of his classes just when he was under suspicion for murder? Who did they think they were fooling? Everyone knew she was the niece of the detective who was heading up the investigation. Did they think she would bat her eyelashes at him, and he would confess? He'd do a lot better than that. He'd teach Pagan Mallory a thing or two.

He picked up a journal on his desk and began to write. Might as well work on his next poetry book. Class didn't start for another few days. Was she in that class? He looked through the lists. Yes, she was. Maybe he would write a poem for her—a poem about roses. Wouldn't that get her going? She'd be out of class and running to her uncle like a shot. He couldn't wait to see the expression on her face. Now, what could he say that was cryptic enough not to get him into trouble? Maybe he would have the entire class write poems about roses. What a hoot! Talk about turning the tables. That would be a day to remember. Maybe the entire class would be put under investigation. He chuckled to himself as a plan began to form in his mind.

The phone call from hell. Let them figure that one out. He grinned at the thought of them scrambling madly about trying to trace his call. They were so dumb. Hadn't he given them enough clues already? He thought of his art—of giving them another one of his creations. No. They didn't deserve it. Not until he saw his poems in print. He would give them until the evening edition before he took some action.

So far, nothing had really touched them. They had only looked at his work as professional observers. He could change that—take them in closer to the action. Then, they might treat him with a little more respect—reverence even. Okay, they had until tonight.

Theo tapped lightly on the office door. "Mal, go home. You've been up twenty-four hours now, and you need your rest. You'll be no good to us if you end up in a hospital bed. We'd have to take time out from the case just to visit you, and you know how crowded that hospital parking can get."

Mallory smiled. "Okay, I surrender. And how about you? You've been here as long as I have. Let me drive you home."

"And who's going to drive you home? Neither one of us need to be driving."

He rubbed his hand across his eyes. "You're right. I'll arrange for one of the patrolmen to give us a lift. Forensics can work better without us getting in their way. The less people here for the next several hours, the better. I am hoping we can keep it from the press until they've finished."

"Do you think someone from the department is involved?"

He gave her a strange look. "You mean do I believe one of us is the killer? I don't believe it, but I have to consider it as a possibility. Look at the lack of usable evidence. That wouldn't be difficult for someone trained in police work."

"But what if forensics doesn't turn up anything?"

"Then, we'll try something else."

"You have a plan, don't you?"

He smiled. "I might. If it's one of us, we'll find him—one way or the other."

Ranoir was already seated when Pagan arrived at the restaurant. He waited until they had ordered before filling her in on what had happened the evening before.

"Then, it can't have been Hardwicke. We've been after the wrong man," she said when he had finished.

"Right now, we're not going to eliminate anybody."

"But how could he have gotten in and out without anyone seeing him."

"It wouldn't have been too difficult. Not many people try to break into a police station. We really aren't on the lookout for that. Most people just walk in."

"But wouldn't someone have noticed?"

"Not necessarily. He could have used a disguise or even posed as one of the cleaning crew."

"But the phone. How did he get into an office and use one of the phones?"

"Maybe he didn't. Maybe he used one of the public phones out front. We just know the call was placed from the station. We don't know which phone was used."

She stared at him for a moment without comment. "You look like hell. Have you been up all night?"

"Most of it. I dozed in the lounge for a few minutes earlier."

"Then, after breakfast, I'm driving you home to get some sleep."

"That won't be necessary. I…"

"Look, I am going to be confronting Hardwicke later, and I need you to watch my back. I would prefer it if you were awake and alert for the job. Now, let's hurry up and eat so you can get some rest."

"And what are you going to be doing while I'm resting?"

"Practicing batting my eyelashes."

CHAPTER 18

▼

Pagan dropped Ranoir off at his apartment and went straight to her uncle's house. With everyone else catching up on their sleep she thought it might be a good time to clean out a few more things from her house trailer. She dropped in and out several times a week, but had not spent any real time cleaning in a while. The "while" being since starting on this case. The work would keep her mind off her upcoming meeting with Hardwicke. A couple of hours should do it.

The Karmann Ghia drove to the gold and white, metal-shuttered travel house like a horse to the feed trough. Maybe she did miss it a little bit. There's something about owning your own place that makes all other places pale in comparison. Or some sentimental claptrap like that. Anyway, she was glad to see the little trailer again.

Walking briskly up the steps, she unlocked the door and opened it wide, granting freedom to all the musky smells that had been forcibly contained for a week. Most of her clothing had already been removed, along with her keepsakes. The leftovers were largely functional. What she had in mind was to remove anything she didn't want and donate it to a local charity. Then, have the vehicle moved into a storage building she had rented some time ago. The items she wanted to carry with her wouldn't take long to pack and load. In an hour's time she was finished and ready to leave.

With the mobile home situation handled, she drove back to her uncle's house, at a loss for filling the remainder of her day. Too bad Ranoir had been up all night because this would be the perfect time to call on Professor Hardwicke. Of course, she hadn't been up all night. How dangerous could it be to meet him in his office? The college was a very public place. He wouldn't dare try anything

- 115 -

there. Why not? Wasn't time of the essence? Her brave action could save some innocent girl's life.

Deciding what to wear to the college for the visual and spiritual seduction of Carl Hardwicke was a lot harder than deciding what to remove from the travel trailer. What would the man like? Short and sassy, long and demure, pants with a smart jacket—the choices could vary greatly. In the end she used logic to make her decision. He liked his students so she needed to dress like one.

Jumping into the Karmann Ghia, she gave little thought to what Ranoir would say when he found out she had gone while he was still asleep—a habit she was finding hard to break. Slipping the key into the ignition, she started the car, and threw it into gear. Two feet later she knew she had a flat. Why now? She was hardly dressed for changing a tire. Maybe she could avoid having to change clothes if she were careful. She had just popped the trunk to remove the jack and spare tire, when she found the note.

The folded sheet of paper had her name written boldly on the front. She unfolded the note and read: *"Pagan. Sorry about the tire. By the time you finish changing it, I should be awake and able to watch your back with Hardwicke."* The message was signed by Ranoir.

She swore under her breath, cursing his name and voicing disparagement on his lineage, while wondering how he had managed to pull this off. The ploy was sneaky and underhanded—worthy of something she might have tried in his place. She walked around to check the tire. Chances were good he hadn't damaged it, but just released the air. That was the kind of act that would fit in with his private code of honor.

Well, if he thought she was going to fix this flat, he had another thing coming. She was facing a couple of tough choices. She could do what he might expect her to do—grab another vehicle and continue with her plan or she could do what he wanted her to do and wait, which would also be the wisest choice. After giving herself a couple of minutes to decide, she went back inside to enjoy another cup of coffee.

Two hours later Demetri arrived at her door. Was a dark gray, silk suit government issue? She didn't think so. And what gave him the right to look so handsome when she was trying to hate him? She invited him in and offered him a drink. He accepted. For the next twenty minutes, he talked about the case and his theories, but not about her flat tire or the fact that she had waited for him. Neither did she—proving that she could not only match his coolness, but also up the ante and raise him one. He was thorough in outlining the parameters within which she was expected to work, emphasizing that at no time was she to put herself into danger.

"Let's take my car," she said with a straight face, as they prepared to leave.

"Mine's all gassed up and ready."

"So is mine."

"Mine's larger."

"But mine's cozier."

He grinned. "Okay, you win. Let's take yours."

Her eyebrows lifted in surprise. She had never expected him to agree. "Yeah, great. Super," she said, the weakness of her rejoinder belying her cheerful words. As he opened the door, she looked back over her shoulder. "We're leaving, Maria," she called, letting the housekeeper know she needed to set the alarm. On the way to the car, she tried to sneak subtle peeks at the tire, while practicing a look of surprise.

Demetri reached his door first, while she circled around the back of the car. By the time she reached her door on the driver's side, practice was unnecessary. To her surprise and amazement the flat tire had been repaired. The blood rushed to her face.

"What's wrong?" he asked as she slid behind the wheel.

Her head snapped around and her eyes flashed, pinning him with a piercing look. "You know damn well what's wrong," she spat with spiraling outrage.

For the space of about a minute their eyes joined and locked—each one of them refusing to give an inch, but then, as if on some prearranged signal, they both burst out laughing. She was the first to speak.

"Where I come from, we have a term for people like you."

"And what would that be?"

She lowered her voice to just above a whisper. "A lady doesn't like to say, but it starts with a 'S' and ends in an 'OB'."

"Ah," he answered, "I think we have the same term where I grew up."

She started the car and backed out of the driveway. "That was a dirty trick. How did you know it would work?"

"I didn't. I just hoped it might slow you down long enough to think about what you were about to do."

She chuckled. "I had time to think, all right. Mostly, I was thinking of all the bad things I'd like to do to you." She stopped there without further explanation, hoping to give him something to think about.

The drive to the college was short, and in the space of fifteen minutes, Pagan was walking down the hall of the Omega building towards Carl Hardwicke's private office. Hunched over his desk, he was scribbling furiously and didn't seem to hear her approach. She stood waiting for a couple of seconds and then, cleared her throat. He turned immediately at the sound.

"Oh, I'm sorry. When I start writing I just shut out the rest of the world. Have you been waiting long?"

His open stare and lilting tone seemed to border on the flirtatious. This was going to be easier than she thought. "No, not at all. I'm sorry to disturb you. I've signed up for your class and wanted to meet you. Were you writing some poetry? I'm a great admirer of your work."

"Are you?"

She nodded and smiled, wondering if she had imagined the subtle hint of sarcasm in his tone. "Oh, yes. I have always loved to read poetry."

"Really? Most young people have little use for reading, much less poetry. Who is your favorite poet?"

She racked her brain for a suitable name. "Uh, Longfellow."

"Hm….Definitely a people's-choice poet. And what poem by him did you particularly like?"

She drew a complete blank. Why hadn't she paid more attention in English class? "'The Raven', " she said, pleased to have come up with a name.

Ranoir cringed on the other end of the wire. No wonder educators were up in arms.

"A very popular selection. I like to see that my students have been studying the Masters. Maybe we could have dinner and discuss some more of his work."

She gave him a beaming smile. "That sounds lovely. I'll meet you back here at your office around seven, if that's all right with you."

"I would be happy to pick you up at your home."

"No, my neighbors love to gossip. I'd rather meet you here."

"Seven, it is then. I'll look forward to it."

He sat outside on the back porch looking toward the old fence. Aged now and damaged in some parts, the old split-tree enclosure had been there for as long as he could remember. He recalled helping his mother repair a portion the morning old man McCally's cow got loose and ran through it. He thought she might be angry because of all the extra work, but he was wrong. She said the cow didn't know any better and that there was no use getting mad at nature. They had spent the afternoon lifting and stacking the long logs. By dusk, the job was finished.

His thoughts returned to the present. The sun was far down in the western sky, telling him that soon the evening papers would be available for sale. He thrilled at the idea of seeing his work in print. Soon, everyone would know of his genius—his greatness. He hoped she knew—that somewhere on some mystic plane of existence she watched him and realized how much he missed her.

Packing his things, he jumped into his car and drove the nearly thirty miles to his in-town apartment. On the way he stopped at a local store to pick up the paper. Not many stores carried the evening paper, but he knew where to stop. He had done his homework on the evening when the first victim was discovered. That time seemed so long ago, now. He couldn't even remember what she looked like or why she had been chosen. The police were probably looking for a connection between the girls, but he was too smart for that.

The clerk gave him change for the one-dollar bill he handed her and made some off-handed remark. He glanced at her nametag. Judy. Nice name, but she wasn't much to look at. Would be though with a little make-up. He could make her look better in death than she had in life. If the poems were there, she would be next. If not, his choice would have to be much more visible—someone guaranteed to involve the paper directly in the case.

He waited until he was in the car before opening to the front page. His work was given top billing. Yes. The bold headline fairly leaped off the page and into the mind's eye. Good coverage, but no poetry. He turned to the second page where the story was continued. Disappointment welled up in his throat like bile, rancid and bitter. Hadn't they believed him? Did they think he was bluffing?

She hung on to things, as if they had the power to define who and what she was—or hoped to become. She was well liked, organized and efficient in her work, and neat in her appearance. Only her house exposed her needy side. Objects, which had been collected obsessively, vied for space and attention in the cluttered rooms. Was it some god's perverse sense of justice that she who collected so much in life should become part of someone else's collection in death?

Rosalynn Springfield moved the brass star paperweight sitting on her desk to the top of the paper stack containing copies of all the articles she could find on the *Rose Murders*. What an interesting case. Too bad she was stuck with the "Dear Rosy" column. In college, she had intended to become an investigative reporter, but when the advice column came open she eagerly accepted the easy work and the steady money the job provided. That was fifteen years ago. But her reporter's nose hadn't completely lost its sense of smell, and right now it told her that something stank big time in the *Rose* case.

Things didn't add up. Didn't the good people of Tyler have a right to know what was going on? When did protecting the integrity of the case cross the line

120   Red Red Rose

defining freedom of information? Weren't sixty thousand minds better than ten or twenty? Why couldn't the community help solve its own crimes? Someone was bound to know something. How many more lives had to be lost before the criminal was brought to justice? Maybe it was time she did some investigating on her own.

When Sergeant Jimmy Jamison checked into the station for his shift, his mood was somber. His unofficial partner, Detective Gail Whiting, had informed him earlier about the telephone call to Van Zandt and how the entire department was being turned upside down. How was he supposed to get any work done like this?

"Morning, Jenkins. Find out anything new on the case?"

"Not since the phone call. Pretty well gives an alibi to DeForest though."

"How do you figure? He could have set the whole thing up. Had one of his pals make the call from a pay phone in here."

Jenkins scratched his chin. "Seems pretty far-fetched to me. If he wanted to do that for an alibi, why didn't he just have the person call from somewhere else? Why would he have him call from here with cops all around?"

"Just to prove he could, Jenkins. You gotta think like a criminal to catch a criminal. They want to prove they are smarter than we are. That's why he did it."

"Maybe, but he's about to be released."

"Damn. Why are they doing that?"

"Cause we can't hold him any longer. That's why. He made bail for the lesser charge last week. We were only holding him on suspicion."

"This is some kind of ruse. I know it is. Where's the Chief?"

"In a meeting. Won't do any good, Jamison. Our hands are tied."

"Maybe, maybe not. He won't get away with this," he finished, turning on his heel to leave.

Chad DeForest followed the guard out of the holding cell and down the hall with a subtle one-finger salute. The sooner he shook the dust from this hellhole off the bottom of his shoes, the sooner he would like it. Paperwork, recovery of valuables, and a brief, but intense lecture about not leaving town colored the rest of his exit, slowing his forward progress to a painful crawl.

Twenty minutes after his initial dismissal from the Tyler City Jail, he was squinting at the setting sun as he made his way down the street to where his parked car was waiting. Traffic was light for early evening causing him to give little thought to the far off sound of a starting engine. Even as the car accelerated, his thoughts were miles away from its noisy approach. With a preliminary glance to gauge the distance, he stopped with both feet on the edge of the curbing and prepared to wait. The possibility of the car jumping the curb never occurred to him. Even as he sailed into the air and hit headfirst into the concrete embankment, the thought refused to register. What the hell had happened? He would never know. The curtain fell on his little play, leaving the epilogue unfinished and the mystery unresolved.

CHAPTER 19

▼

News of the tragedy hit the police station like a brick thrown though a plate-glass window leaving a big mess and a lot of clean up in its wake. No one had seen anything, and no one knew anything, but Mallory was more than sure DeForest's death was no accident. A woman parking her car across the street had heard the whole thing. It was awful. How could such a thing happen right in front of the police station? No, she hadn't seen anything. She had been searching in her purse for her parking ticket when it happened. The car? No, just a dark blur. Could she leave now? She had several errands to run. Hoped they found who did it.

Redford called an immediate meeting in his office. "You know we're going to be crucified over this one, don't you?"

At first no one spoke, then, Jamison's voice boomed from the back of the room, shattering the silence. "They have no right blaming us. The only thing we did wrong was letting him go in the first place. We know for sure he was a rapist and probably the murderer of those poor women. Now, they want us to feel bad cause he's dead? Seems to me we just saved the taxpayers a bunch of money."

The room once again became quiet. "Anyone else have anything to say?" Mallory asked.

Theo stood to her feet. "I understand how Jamison feels. We're all frustrated. We all want an easy answer, but I just don't think DeForest is it. Too many things don't add up. As for his death, I think the first thing we need to determine is whether or not it was intentional or accidental."

Whiting's comment followed as soon as Theo sat down. "I didn't realize there was any question. Do we have any proof it wasn't an accident?"

Mallory stepped forward. "Forensics are working on that now, but we do have some preliminary indication that the car did hit DeForest as he stood on the edge of the curb. Locating the car that was involved is of primary importance. We have had officers around the area asking questions since it first happened. Someone out there knows something. What I want you to do is to uncover a motive. If this was deliberate, then we have a killer out there. Is there a connection between his death and the *Rose Murders*? Check out the families of the victims. Is this a vigilante crime? If you do uncover something you feel to be significant, report to me immediately. Dismissed."

Pagan fought the urge not to run back to the Ghia where she knew Ranoir was patiently waiting. Everything had gone just as she had planned. Let him say something about her detective work now. Inside the car, she discovered Ranoir's expression to be less than overjoyed. Much less.

"What's wrong? I got the date, didn't I? He was completely in my control."

"In your control? He was never in your control, Pagan. He played you from the beginning. Your favorite poet was Longfellow? And by the way, he didn't write 'The Raven.' Poe did. Didn't you take any Lit. classes in high school or college?"

She tossed her head angrily. "I knew Poe wrote 'The Raven.' I just wanted to throw him off, that's all—make him think I wasn't too bright so he would let his guard down."

"Well, in that case, you did just great. I feel sure he doesn't think you're too bright."

"Go ahead. Make fun. When I catch the killer, we'll just see who laughs last. Any news from headquarters?"

"Actually, there was one little thing—Chad DeForest is dead."

"What? How? Tell me what happened."

As he related the facts he had been told regarding DeForest's accident, her face ran the gamut from horrified to relieved. Although she hadn't wanted him dead, she had to admit she felt safer with him off the streets. How could she have ever thought she could be attracted to an animal like that?

Rosalynn walked between the tall rows of books savoring their musty leather scent like the aromatic bouquet of a sweet perfume. Hundreds of pleasurable hours spent in the company of books made any library seem like home. She quickened her step as the magical pull of unread titles caught at her imagination and threatened to detract her from her mission. Ah, to have read full libraries of books—digesting their knowledge—traveling their roads of adventure to new lands—living thousands of lives rather than just one.

The room holding the microfiche was straight ahead. She needed to know everything that had been written on the *Rose Murders*. There had to be something overlooked that would shed some light on the case. She had printed about a dozen articles when she heard the door behind her squeak open. Turning in her chair, she was surprised to see Sergeant Jimmy Jamison walking into the room.

"Sergeant? May I help you?"

"You're from the newspaper, aren't you?" he asked, coming further into the room, his eyes drawn to the articles displayed largely on the screen.

"Why, yes. Have we met?"

"Not formally, but from the articles you're reading, I have the feeling we're here for the same reason."

She glanced back at the screen. "The *Rose Murders*, you mean. I haven't been assigned to them or anything."

"Then, why the research?"

"I don't know. I just have the strangest inkling that we're missing something. Something big."

He watched her for a moment. Maybe there was another way. "What if I could give you an anonymous push in the right direction. Could you keep from revealing your source?"

Her heart was racing, pounding right out of her chest. "Sure, I could. You can help me?"

He looked at the hope etched into her face. It was a homely face—not one made prettier by makeup, but in her eyes he saw something special. Are the eyes the windows of the soul? Hers must surely be pure. "Maybe. Let me see what you have so far."

Pagan dressed that night with special care. What did one wear to expose a murderer? Denim, corduroy, silk? She opted for a rather high fashion little piece she had picked up at Neiman Marcus. That should make his eyes bug out.

The crowded restaurant was a welcome sight after the relative intimacy of Hardwicke's red Mustang convertible. Thank god Tyler's Friday night mentality included a solid tradition of dining out. The old guard, wrapped in their furs, bedazzled in their diamonds, and hairsprayed into coiffeured immobility, waited in lines an hour long in a see-and-be-seen bid for social recognition and one-up-man-ship. As soon as he opened the door, she popped out, smile firmly in place.

"Looks like quite a wait. Would you like a drink from the bar?"

Her smile faltered before she could avoid the involuntary reaction. "Yes, a glass of wine would be nice." As she watched him walk away—picking his way through the fluid mass of hungry people, she speculated about the evening's agenda. Would he try to drug her immediately or wait until the end of the meal?

"Demetri, I hope you're getting this. I'm not volunteering to be victim number six. He's bringing me a drink now." She stopped as she noticed people beginning to turn in her direction. Apparently people who talked to themselves under their breath were considered an oddity in the Rose City. Less than one minute later she spotted Carl weaving through the crowd.

"Your drink," he said, his words announcing his approach.

She took the drink and forced herself to take a sip, as he watched expectantly. Maybe he had already used the drug. How would he explain her unexpected illness? Several reasonable explanations presented themselves, forcing her to admit that removing her from a crowded room wouldn't be much of a problem. The thought was sobering. These people wouldn't question any logical explanation he might give them.

"Follow me. I've located a table."

She stepped in behind him, as the words, "Let the games begin," formed clearly in her mind.

Mallory studied the forensic report for over an hour. At the end of that time he knew little more than he had at the beginning. The word 'inconclusive' summed it up the best. No unexplained prints, no crossed phone wires, and no proof that would tie anyone to the *Rose Murders*. He called Theo's office, thinking she might see something he'd missed.

"Well?" he asked after giving her a few minutes to study the report. "What do you think?"

She lifted her eyes to his. "Like I've said before, the person we're dealing with is bright, clever, cunning, and very confident."

"Do you believe it's an inside job?"

"Yes, I do."

"That leaves me with very little choice."

She knew immediately what he meant. "You're going to run the DNA profiles for comparison."

"I don't have a choice. My back is up against it."

"Isn't that illegal? I thought when the officers participated in the blind study, they were guaranteed confidentiality."

126   Red Red Rose

He cleared his throat. "I'll keep it confidential. I just want to look, that's all—get a possible lead on which direction to take."

"Have you ever written a poem Pagan?"

She stirred the last of her salad. The meal had passed pleasantly enough with little small talk. Now was her chance to pump him for information—cause him to make a slip.

"No, I've just always liked poetry."

"Well, you should try. I recommend starting with a topic with which you are familiar, something local—like roses."

"Roses?" she questioned, her voice sounding high and unnatural.

"Sure—Tyler's claim to fame. I am thinking it would make a good class assignment."

"Rose poems. How interesting."

"Isn't it? I find I have several topics, which seem to recur throughout my writing, like the roses. Death, for instance. I find myself drawn to the subject. What is it called, 'The Undiscovered Country?' I seem to write about death a lot."

"Really?" she prompted, trying to keep the excitement out of her voice. This was it. Her first case and she was on the verge of cracking it open like a walnut.

"Yes, I like to write about young girls—killing them—covering them with red rose petals. What do you think about that?"

She sat immobilized—transfixed—watching his lips say things her ears refused to believe. He seemed not to notice her silence as he continued speaking.

"That's what you've been waiting to hear, isn't it, Miss Pagan Mallory, niece of Chief Detective Augustus Mallory? Anything else you want to know? How did I pick them? Did I enjoy it—get off on it? Did they feel any pain?" He paused to take a sip of wine. "So, are you wired?" he asked in a quieter voice. "Is your partner getting all of this down? I hope so because I'm getting pretty fed up with the harassment."

Pagan released a long, slow breath she had been unaware of holding.

"What? Cat got your tongue? Are you going to try to cuff me? Did you think I wouldn't recognize your name?" He leaned forward. "Listen, if I had done it, would I have been stupid enough to leave the one clue that would tie me to the murders?"

"How did you know about the poems?" she asked, finally finding her voice.

"One of your buddies on the force spilled the beans—accused me of doing the writing."

"Who? Give me a name."

"Why should I? The poem theory is all you've got, sugar. Lots of guys dated Carla. I was just one of the bunch. Not enough evidence for a conviction and you know it. You've got nothing."

"What about Nancy Starnes? How did you know her?"

His eyes narrowed. "How did you know about that?"

She decided to level with him. "Your picture was on her wall—in the painting."

Her words produced an unexpected effect. He looked away, and his face crumpled.

"Her mother and I were married for two years. She was my stepdaughter."

Pagan sat non-pulsed, stunned by his words, and unsure of how to proceed. He wasn't the killer—her every instinct told her that. "I'm sorry. I didn't know."

"When I first met her she was six or seven. Such a sweet child. We kept in touch through the years—she called me just last month. Her death was a shock."

Rosalynn read through the poems one more time. What a gold mine. When she brought these to the paper, they would have to move her to reporting. What they had before on the case had been interesting. The poems would elevate it to riveting, maybe even rating national coverage. She opened her laptop and began to type.

Pagan walked into the parking lot and waited. Nothing had gone as she had planned, and to top it all off, she had been dumped at the restaurant and stuck with the bill. Now what? Were they back to square one? As Demetri pulled the car alongside her, she wondered how this would effect their previous agreement. She had done as he demanded and posed as bait. Shouldn't that mean her debt was paid in full?

"Well, I guess, that's that?"

Demetri waited until she had buckled her seatbelt before responding to her comment.

"What do you mean? Are you assuming Hardwicke has been cleared?"

"Yes, aren't you. He explained why his picture was on her wall."

"Maybe. Maybe not."

"What do you mean?"

"He just explained that he already knew her. He didn't explain about the picture."

She was puzzled. "I don't get it. I thought the reason we suspected Hardwicke was his picture in the painting. He explained that, so he's off the hook."

He pulled the car into the long line of traffic. "No, we suspected him because he was on very familiar terms with, at least, two of the victims. Were you unaware that he had been married to Nancy's mother?"

She turned in her seat. "Are you telling me you already knew?"

"Yes, the entire team did."

She couldn't believe her ears. "Then, why didn't someone say anything to me?"

"The information was in the report, which you should have been studying. If you had, you would have known he was Nancy's former stepfather."

She stared at his profile through the alternating shadowed glow of the streetlights and passing headlights. "You let me go into a potentially dangerous situation unprepared," she accused.

"How was I supposed to know you were unprepared?"

"You knew. Why did you do it?"

He changed lanes and pulled out onto the loop before answering. "All right. I did suspect you hadn't bothered to read the report. Your error. If you want to get involved in detective work, you have to be prepared. You need to learn that. Also, I had your back. You were in no danger. Finally, your ignorance gave him the idea that we were about twenty steps behind him and not too bright. Overconfidence leads to mistakes."

"And what if he's telling the truth?"

"Then, good for him. We will look further."

They didn't speak again until he pulled into her drive to drop her off. "Look," he said. "Despite not doing your homework, your questions were good."

"Right."

"No, really. You have the instincts of a good detective."

She got out of the car. "Thanks," she said, before slamming the door.

CHAPTER 20

▼

Rosalynn was right. The newspaper was thrilled, and advanced her immediately to the position of lead reporter on the story. Augustus Mallory was less enthusiastic. He was at home when the first calls started coming in.

"Detective Mallory, this is Steve Harmon from the Tyler Times Courier. We have recently discovered a series of poems that, according to our sources, were uncovered with the bodies. Do you have any comment on why this information was withheld from the public?"

Mallory listened in disbelief. Someone close to the case had leaked confidential information—maybe even the killer himself. "I have no comment at this time."

The line had barely disconnected when the second call came through. This time it was from the station. He listened, growing increasingly agitated. "Refer all answers to me, Whiting. No one is to comment on the poetry or any other aspect of the case. Is that clear? I'll be down shortly."

He grabbed his coat and headed out, passing Pagan on his way to the door.

"What's up?" she asked, reading the consternation on his face.

"The papers have copies of the poems."

"How?"

"That's what I hope to find out. Could be the break we've been waiting for."

When Mallory arrived at the station, the time was after eleven p.m. Because it was Friday night, he had expected to see a lot of activity, but nothing could have prepared him for the throng of reporters and television crews that descended on him as soon as he left the car.

"Any comment on the *Rose Murder* poet?"

130   Red Red Rose

"Why was this information withheld from the public?"

"What else are the police hiding?"

"Are you close to an arrest?"

Mallory bulldozed his way to the station door, where Chief Redford met him.

"It's been like this for over an hour. The Mayor is demanding an explanation and an arrest."

"Does he have anyone particular in mind or will anyone do?"

Redford led the way to his office, his tall, thin form dominating the narrow hallway. "At this point, I think he would settle for anyone. According to him, the voters are up in arms. Do you have any suspects besides Hardwicke?"

Mallory followed the Chief into his office, closing the door behind him. "As a matter of fact, this leak may prove to be our first big break."

"What do you mean?"

"Give me an hour."

Redford looked as if he were going to refuse. "The Mayor is waiting for my call. All right, one hour, then I need an answer."

Mallory obtained a copy of the duty roster from Jenkins before calling Whiting into his office.

"Sir?"

"Locate the team and call them in."

"Already been on it, sir. Got hold of everyone but Jamison. He's probably visiting his mother."

Mallory looked up in surprise. "His mother?"

"Yeah, he said she lives alone, so he stops by frequently to look in on her."

"Do you have a number for her?"

"No. He never listed one."

"Okay. Keep trying to locate him. Is Theo here?"

"Yes, sir. Arrived just before you."

"Good. Please ask her to stop in."

"Sure. Anything else?"

"Let me know when you reach Jamison."

Mallory opened the case file, looking for anything he might have missed. When Theo came in, he was still looking.

"Here is a copy of the paper," she said, placing the evening edition in front of him on the desk. "I looked at it earlier. Everything is there, but one of the poems has a misprint."

He opened the paper to the section containing the poems. "Where?"

She walked around to look over his shoulder. "There, that one," she said, pointing at the page. "It reads:

> And as the light fades from your eyes—
> Your warm skin growing cold,

Where it should read:

> And as the light fades from your eyes—
> Your warm skin growing old,"

Mallory located the copy of the poem inserted in the folder. Theo was right, there was a discrepancy. Still…. "Theo would you bring me the original poem from the evidence room? Something's not right."

"Sure. Want to tell me what?"

"Not just yet, but I have a hunch."

Theo returned almost immediately with the plastic bag containing the poems. He opened it almost reverently and pulled out the poem from the Nancy Starnes murder. The lines jumped out at him almost immediately:

> "And as the light fades from your eyes—
> Your warm skin growing cold,"

Theo watched his face for some clue to what he was thinking. "Did you find something?"

"Look here," he said, turning the pages toward her. "The poem in our report contained a typo. The letter 'c' was left out, changing 'cold' to 'old', but the poem in the paper didn't match our report. It matched the original."

"Okay. So what does that mean?"

He smiled. "It means we are going to run the DNA test on the members of the department and see if we have a match. That reporter interviewed either someone with access to the evidence room or the killer himself. We'll conduct the interview first thing tomorrow morning."

When Pagan entered the kitchen the next morning, Maria was already laying out steaming plates of eggs, bacon, biscuits, and gravy. Pagan paused when she spotted the fourth place setting. "Is someone joining us for breakfast, Maria?"

"Agent Ranoir. He's talking with your uncle in his office right now."

132   Red Red Rose

Hell's bells. What was that man up to now? More importantly, what was he saying to her uncle? "Knock, knock," she said, opening the door to her uncle's office. "May I come in?"

Her uncle looked up and smiled. She didn't dare look at Demetri. "Sure, Agent Ranoir was just telling me how much help you have been to him."

Caught off guard, she took her seat before attempting any sort of reply. "We have made some progress," she said, keeping her comment neutral.

"He said you both feel the case against Hardwicke to be weak."

She shot a quick look toward Demetri. He was looking straight at her, waiting for her reaction. "Yes, he seemed to be genuinely broken up over Starnes's death as well as that of his sometime girlfriend, Carla Clumb. Add the poems to the mix and he appears to have been set up."

"Ranoir said you are showing good instinct for the work."

She didn't allow herself a reaction. "So, if he didn't do it, who did? Do we have any other suspects?"

"I have a couple of ideas. Tomorrow I'd like you and Ranoir to interview the press. Find out who gave them the poems along with a good description of the person. Don't take 'no' for an answer."

"You think the killer himself might have given her the poems?"

"I'll let Ranoir fill you in, but in a word, 'yes.' I think it is very possible."

The newspaper was reluctant to talk. With a source this well placed they were looking at years of insider information—or so they thought. Getting to Rosalynn took an act of God. Ranoir intimidated and threatened his way past the reporters straight through to the editor and then stalled. He spent two hours convincing the man that if his lack of cooperation resulted in another murder, he would be charged with obstructing justice and blamed for the death of an innocent girl. His argument worked, and Ranoir was given the name Rosalynn Springfield.

The rest should have been easy. However, Rosalynn, expecting the editor to give her up, had hidden in an out of the way hotel to avoid being questioned. She might have remained hidden had not the television picked up the story, and plastered her photograph all over the news. Once reporters cited her as the key to solving the case of the *Rose Murders*, her anonymity was over. The hotel manager called the 1-800 number he saw listed on the screen and told everything he knew.

Ranoir and Pagan arrived at her room a few minutes after the call came in. The room was shoddy, cheap, and ratty looking with faded pink-flowered wallpaper—the kind of room most patrons paid for by the hour. Rosalynn had asked her editor for advice, and he told her to talk. Not worth jail time, he said. This is

FBI, and these guys mean business. So she talked. Told how she had met him at the library—described him—offered to come down to the station. Told them everything they wanted to know, except the most important thing of all—his name and that he was a policeman.

"Did he tell you how he knew about the existence of the poems?"

"No."

"Then, why did you believe him?"

She thought for a minute. "Because he produced them, and his story rang true."

Pagan interrupted with a question of her own. "Didn't it ever occur to you that you might be talking to the killer?"

"No," she answered immediately.

"Why not?"

"Well, I don't know. He just didn't seem to be the sort."

Ranoir took a step forward, getting right up in the woman's face. "Wasn't the reason that he didn't seem to be a murderer due to the fact he was wearing a policeman's uniform?"

Mallory knew the DNA comparison would take time, and that the evidence might prove to be inconclusive. Still, it might point them in the right direction. At this point, he felt he had nothing to lose. He had arrived at the station early, feeling a sense of urgency at the possible ending of the case. To his surprise, Theo was already there.

"Great minds think alike," was her answer to his questioning look.

"How about 'the early bird gets the worm?'"

"I wish I had the proverbial 'worm' right now, but the DNA comparison isn't ready yet."

"How much longer?"

She shrugged. "They won't say."

"Hm…." was all he said, looking vaguely across the room.

She looked at him sharply. "You think you know who it is, don't you?"

CHAPTER 21

▼

"Jimmy, Jimmy, are you in there?"

"Gail, what are you doing here?"

"Oh, good. I have been trying to reach you since last night. Did you see the poems in the paper? Someone leaked them to the press. Mallory thinks that when he discovers who talked to the reporter he will find out who the killer is. Won't that be great?"

He nodded. "Yes, that will be wonderful."

She walked through the door and looked around. "This is your mother's house, isn't it? I'd like to meet her."

"I'd like that, too. Maybe in a bit. She's resting now."

Gail moved further into the room. "You grew up in this house, didn't you? It looks abandoned. Is your mother an invalid?"

He walked over to stand behind her. "No, not really. Would you like something to drink?"

"Sure, I guess so. This house is like stepping back in time."

He laughed. "Funny you should put it like that. I always get the same feeling. Mother loves it here. Those are her rose bushes outside. She cares for her roses like they are her kids. The red ones are her favorites."

She followed him into the kitchen. The room was clean—maybe too clean—almost sterile. Certainly not warm and cozy the way a kitchen should be. She couldn't picture his mother or any woman cooking in the room. He seated her at a small wooden breakfast table, and walked across the room to make the tea.

"Tell me about growing up here, Jim. Was it just you and your mother?"

"I had a friend," he said, placing the kettle on the stove, "who lost his mother at an early age." As Gail watched, Jimmy struck a match to light the gas burner. With the water ready to heat, he opened the side cabinet and reached for two mismatched China cups before resuming his narrative. "His father had died before he was born, so he and his mother were naturally very close. They were each other's whole world." He paused to bring the cups to the table, then moved over to look out the window. His voice was low as he continued, causing her to sit forward, straining to catch every word. "One day, when the young boy was about ten years old, he and his mother were up on the widow's walk playing a game, as they often did. She got closer to the edge than she had realized and started to lose her balance. Terrified that she would fall, he ran over to give her a hand. That's when the unimaginable happened. Just as he reached her, his foot caught on a stone and he tripped, knocking her over the edge of the roof. Screaming her name, my friend watched in disbelief as she disappeared over the side of the short wall. The dull thud that followed didn't prepare him for the sight of her lifeless body, bloody and broken on the ground below or for the awful silence that followed. He ran down the gray stone steps two at a time and gathered her into his arms. That's the way they were when a neighbor found them late that evening." Jamison turned from the window, his face empty. "Do you take sugar in your tea?" he asked.

Mallory read the report over and over until the words swam in front of his eyes. "Suspecting" is the cool logic of analysis. "Knowing" is the horror of truth. The cleanly typed pages confirmed his worst suspicions. The DNA match belonged to Jimmy Jamison. His mind raced for some explanation to refute what he knew in his heart to be true. Jimmy Jamison was a murderer.

He found Ranoir and Pagan in the workroom, plying Rosalynn Springfield with mug books. He passed them by and went straight up to the would-be reporter. "Was Sergeant Jimmy Jamison your source?"

Her eyes opened until he thought they would pop out of her head, but she answered in the negative.

Mallory took her by the arms, and asked again. The atmosphere in the room was tense, as everyone waited to see if she would admit to what Mallory already seemed to know. "We have his DNA on one of the victims. You are helping a murderer to go free. Now, tell me the truth. Was it Jamison?"

Rosalynn started to cry—first in tiny streams, then in a wailing river. "Yes, it was Jamison. Oh my god. I helped the man who killed those poor girls. I was alone with him. I published his poems. Oh my god."

Mallory let her go. "Pagan, Ranoir, get someone for her, and then meet me in my office. Let's keep a lid on this for now. Our killer is still out there."

By the time they reached the office, everyone else was in place except for Whiting and Jamison.

"Has anyone heard from Gail?" Mallory asked, looking over the team.

"She was going to talk to Jamison," Theo volunteered. "She thought he might be visiting his mother."

"Allison Jamison is dead. She died when he was ten in a tragic accident. He blamed himself. Grew up in an orphanage, had a spotless record at the academy, and has had an exemplary police career. However, all of our evidence points to him as the killer. I know this is hard, but we have to bring him in and protect Whiting. Send a unit to his apartment. We'll start looking at the house where his mother died."

Gail's eyes welled up in sympathy and understanding. "It wasn't your fault, Jimmy. It was an accident. Can't you see that? Your mother wouldn't want you to blame yourself."

His eyes were strange when he looked at her. "I see her, you know. Falling…falling…and I scream her name over and over."

She murmured something else, but he didn't seem to hear. "I miss her so much. Mama, Mama. Why did you leave me?"

As Gail watched helplessly, the man she had worked beside for two years unraveled right before her eyes. The demons, which had tortured him in secret, were now in full control. She sat unmoving as he turned and ran toward the set of stairs at the end of the room. By the time she could force herself to follow, the upstairs door was closed and locked. She ran to the car for her police radio and placed a call to the station. Dispatch connected her to Mallory, who was in route. She outlined the situation.

Mallory pulled up just as Jamison stepped out of the attic window onto the widow's walk. He slammed to a stop, grabbing the foghorn from the back seat as he exited the vehicle. "Come down, Jamison. Let's talk. We can help you."

Jamison seemed to be listening. "Can you bring her back?"

"We can send you to someone who can help you."

"But can you bring her back to me?"

Mallory motioned the team around the side of the building. They hoped to reach the stairs before anything happened.

"No, Jamison, but you will get the help you need."

"But I need her," he said, walking nearer to the edge.

Mallory lifted the horn once again as Gail stepped through the upstairs window onto the roof. Jamison never noticed. Time stood suspended and looped back on itself while the cries of a ten-year old boy blended with those of a grown man. Then it was over, as a story that began years ago came to a poetic end, and Jimmy Jamison jumped off the widow's walk, ending his torment forever.

The funeral was held three days later with national coverage. Many members of the police department attended in an official as well as an unofficial capacity. Gail Whiting wept openly for a grieving ten-year-old boy, for the disturbed man he had become, and for the victims left behind.

"Why did he do it?" Pagan asked her uncle when it was over.

"Why does anyone kill?"

"But this case was different. He had suffered so much pain."

"Everyone suffers, Pagan, but only a few people ease their pain by causing pain to others. If we knew why, maybe we could eliminate killing altogether."

Ranoir joined Mallory as he headed back to the car. "I have to be back in Washington tomorrow morning."

"Just when I was getting used to having you around."

Ranoir grinned. "I'll try not to stay away too long. I feel like I should return for the Rose Festival, at least." He took a step back to walk with Pagan who was following behind them. "Would you let me take you to dinner tonight? There's something I'd like to talk to you about."

She nodded. "I'll be ready by seven."

Demetri arrived early, while Pagan came down predictably late, having gone through several changes of clothing before choosing a demure, pastel sundress. As she closed the door of her room, she saw him waiting for her at the foot of the stairs. Gone was the harsh, demanding agent she had worked with for the past few weeks. In his place was a dark, handsome knight, ready to sweep her off her feet.

"I've made reservations for us at the Starlight Dinner Club, if that's all right with you," he said, winking with a smile that made her heart turn somersaults.

"Sounds great." Was this the same man that had bullied her, taunted her, and made her life hell? Somehow the frog had turned into the handsome prince. She allowed him to lead her to the car, all the while, waiting for the other shoe to drop.

The beginning of the evening was formal and awkward, but by the end they were talking like old friends. Intense situations either bind people together or split them wide apart. She, however, was unconvinced. After a couple of glasses of wine and several romantic dances, she voiced the question uppermost in her mind. "All right, Ranoir. Why the moonlight and magnolias? Why did you really ask me out?"

He leaned down to plant a light kiss on the tip of her nose. "I enjoy your company."

"And?"

"I wanted to see you apart from the case—socially."

"And?"

"You still doubt my motives?"

"Let's call it a hunch."

He gave a low chuckle. "I told you your instincts were good."

She accepted the compliment, but remained wary. "What do you want?"

Again, the engaging smile. "Well, there is this one little thing that I had hoped you could help me with."

"And what would that be?"

"I need some private investigating done by someone I can trust in an unofficial capacity."

"And you think you can trust me?"

His voice lowered to a more serious tone. "I would trust you with my life."

"On what do you base this confidence?"

"Let's just say I have some good instincts of my own."

She smiled in response, not intending to give him an answer right away. A girl needs information and time to weigh her options. But whatever she might decide about the job, she knew one thing for sure. She knew what she liked, and she liked what she saw. Trust her instincts? A feeling down deep inside told her this relationship was far from over. She would take the job—get to know this man, and if her instincts were even half way right, be a key player in an adventure that had only just begun.

"To our instincts," she said, raising her glass of wine in salute.

"To our instincts," he echoed, raising his own glass and sealing a pact that would take them both further than they had ever wanted or expected to go.

The End.

COMING SOON...

DARK LEGACY

"Wake, up blondie. Do you hear me, Kate? Wake up!" The burly man shook his head disgustedly and walked over to join his companion.

Kate half turned, her blonde hair spilling over her cheek, but her eyes remained tightly closed. Scenes of childhood danced in her mind taking her back to more peaceful times.

"Was that Gran calling? No, Gran would never have referred to her as Kate. Her grandmother had reared Kate and, of course, her mother, but unlike her namesake in *The Taming of the Shrew*, her real name was Katherine.

"How long is the drug supposed to last?"

"Not sure. We gave her a pretty strong dose. Who'd figure she'd be such a hellcat?"

"We could at least untie her."

"No way. You didn't receive the benefit of her claws or her knee before she passed out. Tied up suits me just fine," he finished, aiming a menacing kick at Kate's still sleeping form. The men walked out of the warehouse, leaving their unconscious captive behind.

Kate stirred slightly as the cold from the concrete floor began to seep through the red silk blouse she was wearing. The cold reminded Kate of Aspen, of smooth mountain slopes, and of Stephen. The last thought warmed her in spite of the cold. Kate stirred again, but this time tiny sparks of awareness began to filter through. She groaned softly, unconsciously protesting the tightly bound rope cutting into her wrists and ankles.

Katherine Elizabeth Dubois was well proportioned in spite of her small stature and rather slender build, and the unlined innocence of her face belied her almost twenty-five years. She stirred once again and then lay still.

Outside the warehouse Kate's abductors waited impatiently. The one called Jack checked his watch and spat out a string of expletives.

"I thought he'd be here by now." Jack kicked at the tire of the car they were using for this caper. It was old, dirty enough to go unobserved, and brown enough in color so as to appear beyond description. The men were also somewhat ordinary. The police report, were there to have been a police report, would have read something like this: medium height, medium build, brown hair, brown eyes, no distinguishing characteristics.

Jack threw down his cigarette and lit another. "How much longer are we gonna have to wait. We got her here, and I need my money."

His companion answered him; "You'd better be glad he's late and hope he waits 'til she's awake. Unharmed, remember. He wants her unharmed."

"Yeah…yeah. You should have remembered before you shot her up."

What a pleasant dream she was having. Stephen Johns…. He was as fair-haired as she was, but where her eyes were sky blue, his were sea green. At first glance, they looked more like brother and sister than like friends. Not that Kate didn't hope for a deeper relationship. Kate smiled as she sighed unconsciously. The dream seemed clearer now. The sun was beaming down unmercifully on the unending white of the slopes. Stephen stood like some young Norse god with his blonde hair, his blue ski jacket, and his striking good looks. A ski instructor cliché'.

She didn't really expect him to notice her among all the young butterfly debutantes fluttering around him. Although to be truthful, without being overly immodest, she knew that most men considered her pleasing to the eye, if not glamorous. She could still remember how she felt as she saw him surrounded by all the young hopefuls. She was just one among many and had just reached the edge of the ski group, when, as if in slow motion, Stephen turned from the eager, smiling faces vying for his attention and made his way toward her.

"Ahaa…" Kate caught her breath as she felt a sharp pain in her side. "That wasn't supposed to happen," she thought. She tried to move her hand to her side. Something was wrong, she couldn't move her hand. She couldn't even feel her hand. Except for the pain, her whole body felt numb.

"Wake up, sweetheart." A foot scraped menacingly over the concrete floor as if positioning itself for another strike.

"Let me try. You'll break her ribs." Jack shook Kate gently, "Kate, its time to wake up. Come on, Kate. I know you can hear me." Jack paused, watching Kate closely.

Kate tried to shrink inside herself and become very small. Mostly, she just tried not to move.

Jack stroked her arm as he continued, "The choice is yours, Kate. Either wake for me or wake for Pete.

"Some girls really go for the rough stuff." Jack stood slowly to his feet. "Funny, I didn't pick you as one of them."

Kate tried to open her eyes. They felt glued together or maybe sealed with hot wax. What was wrong with her? She tried harder. Slowly, she began to pick up light, fuzzy light and fuzzy shadow. Where was she? She began to look around and, then, stopped. Her eyes paused at the two shadows standing beside her head, while her brain screamed warnings.

"Thought that might bring you 'round," said the voice that had spoken to her before. "Now we'll just wait quietly for your Prince Charming to come to your rescue." He winked at the man beside him and both men laughed.

Kate lay unmoving and let the memories slowly come back to her as consciousness returned. Was it just this morning that she had dressed so carefully for work, wanting to look good for the new boss at the department store? Everything at work had gone smoothly. The new boss had made a great first impression, especially on the female clerks.

After work she had stayed a few minutes late to close out the books. When she entered the car park, it was dark. Kate had worked late on several occasions and, therefore, had no reason to be alarmed.

When the man first grabbed her from behind, she was too stunned to react. She offered no resistance for the first few seconds. Strong arms surrounded her in a vice-like grip and dragged her off to the right. Kate felt herself being pushed into a vehicle where another man was waiting. Her stupor ended and she began to fight. She remembered the feeling now, as something exploding inside her brain, inciting all her body's moving parts to flail wildly in all directions.

Kate remembered nothing beyond that point. Apparently, she'd been knocked out or drugged. Why?

She tried to think, but quickly became content with staring vacantly. Her brain wasn't really working yet, and her body was too tired to make the effort.

Jack watched Kate as she struggled to come to terms with her captivity. Satisfied that she was secured and would pose no problem, he joined Pete outside the warehouse.

"Any sign of him yet?"

"No, not yet. I think…." Pete's voice faded as both men picked up the sound of a high powered engine becoming increasingly louder.

Jack was the first to react, "I think our wait is over. All that's left is the green. 'Bout time, too. I'm not used to having to wait for my cash."

The sleek, low-slung sports car pulled up to the warehouse, and its door flew open almost the moment it stopped.

"Where's the girl?" Ramon Escarté was skilled in making even a simple inquiry sound like a royal command. Most men found him to be intimidating,

142   Red Red Rose

even though his height of six feet wasn't unusual and his medium build, though well developed, wasn't imposing. Ramon had the look of a panther, ready to strike.

Women, on the other hand, saw Ramon in an entirely different light. To them, he had a dark sensual look that quickened the pulse at a glance and stirred the imagination. They felt power flow from him, just as their male counterparts, but where the men perceived a threat, the women knew a promise.

Both Jack and Pete approached the red corvette with caution. Pete gestured toward the inside of the warehouse.

"She's inside—unharmed. But where's the guy we made the contract with and where's the dough?"

Ramon stepped from the car. "You'll get your money from me when I get the girl—unharmed." His emphasis on the last word was unmistakable.

Ramon led the two men into the relative dimness of the warehouse, pausing momentarily inside the door as his eyes adjusted to the subdued light. When he spotted Kate tied up on the floor, his face became set and his eyes hard. "You fellas never heard of shock? She's like ice. We specified that she must be delivered unharmed. A little longer and she might not even have been delivered alive."

Pete began to protest, "But we only...."

"Don't bother making excuses. Just take your money and go."

The two men moved quickly away. They were only too glad to pick up the envelopes containing their payment and distance themselves from their employer, a man they could only think of as dangerous. A cloud of dust filled the air as their car sped away.

Ramon sat Kate down in the passenger seat in the Corvette and began to untie her wrists. Kate continued to stare blankly ahead—not really aware of what was happening to her. She showed no real signs of life until Ramon began to massage her wrists and ankles. As the blood began to circulate, sharp stabbing pains filled her mind and her body. She groaned and twisted slightly.

Ramon stopped his ministrations and reached for a blanket in the back seat. He began to spread it across her now shivering body, fastened her seatbelt, and closed her door. She turned her head to watch him as he approached the driver's side of the car. He melted into the car in one smooth, fluid motion as driver and car became as one.

Kate tried to gather her thoughts and make some kind of sense of what was happening to her. "Who are you?" She ventured weakly.

Ramon gave her a mocking look. "Let's just say that you're the fairy princess, I'm your shining knight, and I'm taking you to the castle to meet the queen." With that, he turned back to the road, leaving her to make of it what she would.

Kate wasn't up to riddles. She settled back in the seat and filled her mind with the lullaby of road sounds made by the car.

****

C Rowe–Myers—crowemyers22@hotmail.com

0-595-30266-1

LaVergne, TN USA
30 September 2009
159438LV00002B/4/A